CRIME AND NOURISHMENT

BOOK 1: ANGIE PROUTY NANTUCKET COZY MYSTERY SERIES

MIRANDA SWEET

HIDDEN KEY PUBLISHING

"It is a good phrase that," said Poirot. "The impossible cannot have happened, therefore the impossible must be possible in spite of appearances."

—Murder on the Orient Express

Chapter 1

PASTRIES & PAGE-TURNERS

Angie leaned her ancient gray bicycle against the side of the bookstore. On the one side was a flower box full of pink geraniums; on the other, the freshly painted teal front door, standing out against the gray shingles of the rest of the building. A bronze ship's bell hung on the doorframe and a blue whale-shaped sign announced the name of the store: Pastries & Page-Turners. All that was missing was the smell of roasting coffee, which she would rectify in a few minutes.

Inside the front window, underneath a display of pirate-themed books, scowled Captain Parfait, a tortoiseshell cat with a scar over one eye, a ragged ear, and a limp. He was impatient for breakfast after a hard night guarding the bookshop from thieves, mice, and late-night tourists.

She unlocked the door. On the front mat was a pair of bookmarks with their fuzzy gray bobbles gnawed off. If Captain Parfait couldn't *find* a mouse, he'd *make* one. Or two. Sometimes she swore he was the reincarnation of her obstinate great-grandfather, Captain John F.

Prouty. Fortunately, she could stand the loss of a couple of bookmarks now and then, in order to satisfy her hunter-kitty's mighty pride.

She picked up the disemboweled bookmarks, gave Captain Parfait a scratch behind the ear, and took a quick whiff: nothing but good, rich bookstore smell.

Which made leaving her old investment firm in Manhattan and returning home to Nantucket *more* than worth it.

It was going to be a good day.

Angie fed Captain Parfait, started the coffee, checked the refrigerators, and started unpacking the big boxes of books she'd received in the mail yesterday. Most of these were special orders that would have to be delivered later, after her great-aunt Margery came in for the day. Aunt Margery (she claimed to be too humble and too not-Russian to answer to the title "great") would watch the store while Angie delivered books around the island.

About elbow-deep in the second box, the back door opened with a "Hey, twinkle toes!" as the pastries—the other half of the Pastries & Page-Turner's business model—arrived, along with Angie's best friend, Josephine.

Jo was the shorter, green-haired half of the Jerritt twins—the other one being her brother, Mickey. The two of them ran The Nantucket Bakery on Main Street, and every morning Jo bicycled around town with a cart full of croissants, cheesecake, cookies and more; delicacies that filled up Angie's refrigerator case and lured tourists in off the street.

"Hello!" Angie shouted. "I'm back in the stock room."

Jo leaned around the doorframe. Her pale eyebrows were pinched together in the center so hard that it left a red spot. "You hear?"

"Hear what?"

"It ain't good. Come help me unload. You're not gonna believe it."

Angie followed her outside and picked up three flat plastic boxes marked with *P&P* in permanent marker on top. "Don't keep me in suspense."

"It's Snuock. He's raising the rent, starting August first. By a lot. I mean, a *lot*."

Angie blinked. "What?"

Alexander Snuock was the infamous miser who owned half the island; not only had his family lived here for generations, but he rarely emerged from the mansion on top of the hill where he'd hidden for the last twenty years. He wasn't broke and didn't need the money—and for several of the small businesses in the area, a rent increase could mean going out of business.

"Snuock stopped by this morning to give us the news...I think he just wanted to see us squirm in person. He could have sent an email or something. My guess is that he's on his way here soon...I'd get ready, if I were you."

Angie's gut clenched. "How...much?"

"He says he's calculating it by square foot. Ours just went up seven hundred bucks per month."

Angie did a quick mental guesstimate. "So mine should be about five hundred dollars. Per month. That's crazy."

"You're telling me," Jo said.

Angie felt stunned. The plans she'd made to take a week off in January to go to Greece were rapidly melting away.

"Who else?"

"Oh, a lot of people. Ruth next door to you, for one."

"That's terrible," Angie said.

Jo walked back outside and Angie followed her. Getting back on her bike, Jo said, "Sorry I can't stay to chat, but I gotta get a move on before Snuock gets here. Ma offered to help us with the extra cash, but Mickey and I agreed that we weren't gonna lean on her for help. We're just gonna have to make up with extra sales over the Fourth."

It was Thursday, the third of July, and tomorrow Angie would set up a bookstore tent at the festival on Main Street—the entire street would be closed off downtown for pedestrians, food and sales tents, and a huge water fight in the evening—with clam bakes, sailing tours, and fair rides elsewhere near the beach.

Making an extra buck always seemed easy in the summer, when the island was covered in tourists, but the winter months would drain the bakery, and they both knew it.

"I'll keep an ear out for anyone else interested in selling pastries. Or who needs catering."

"I know you already do, babe," Jo said. "Hugs and kisses for Aunt Margery and the captain. Mickey says if he gets a minute, he'll stop in later. Ta."

~

Almost immediately after Jo left, Alexander Snuock showed up at the back door with a sharp rap of the knuckles and a genial call of, "So how's my favorite bookseller this morning?"

Angie wouldn't have been surprised if he'd waited along a side street for Jo to hop back on her bicycle and pedal away.

"I'm your *only* bookseller," she said. Normally she was able to say the words with some lightness to her voice. This morning she seemed to taste ashes in her mouth.

"Oh," Snuock said, coming through the door, voice oozing with fake sympathy. "You just heard the news. Your rent's going up."

Snuock wore an expensive, tailored suit, pale gray with a blue-and-yellow striped tie, and a matching blue pocket squire. He wore burgundy wing-tip oxfords and a silver Rolex watch.

Angie took a deep breath. "How much?"

"You'll get the paperwork after the holiday, but, as I recall, it's approximately five hundred dollars. Less than five-ten." He frowned at her, a face full of concern that was just as insincere as his smile. "Come on, Angie. You know you can afford it. You *know* that you were getting a far, far better deal on the property than any other owner on the island would have given you. Costs rise. You've had your window of grace to get your business started. Don't tell me that you don't have the money to cover what is a completely fair increase.

She swallowed. Even though she had the impulse to argue with Snuock and set him straight about his distorted definition of fair, she wasn't going to; he'd likely just raise the rents even higher. She did have some money tucked away—a slight comfort. But it still bit, and bit hard.

Snuock walked over to the coffee pots and poured himself a cup of coffee, adding cream and grabbing a pastry from Jo's tray. He took a sip, then a bite of the pastry.

"Excellent," he said. Then closed his eyes and took a deep breath. "You know how much I love coming into used bookstores and taking a whiff of the pages. It's a particular pleasure of mine. I should stop by here more often." If he did, he'd do nothing but chase the locals away.

He took another bite of pastry, the crumbs stuck to the ends of his mouth.

Then Angie, in her most friendly, customer-service voice, said: "Mr. Snuock, that coffee and pastry will be six twenty-five." She couldn't help herself; she wouldn't argue or yell, but she could make a point. "I'm sure you understand, with the rents going up and all."

His eyes popped opened and he practically choked; he was used to everyone kowtowing to him.

A thin, stiff smile spread across his face as he dug in his back pocket for his wallet and handed over the cash.

He cleared his throat. "Have my books arrived yet?"

"Not yet," Angie said, placing the money in the till. "And I haven't had a chance to open the packages that came in earlier."

"If they have, bring them up to me right away," Snuock said, regaining his composure. "Ah! Well, I have to keep moving." He raised his coffee cup toward her and headed toward the back door.

Angie was relieved that he was leaving; it was all she had been able to do to keep from shouting at him. Then she heard someone else approaching the back door of the bookstore, angry footsteps that scattered pebbles through the parking lot.

Oh no. There were probably at least a dozen angry business owners in the area looking to vent their troubles and drink coffee this morning...it really was inevitable that one of them would show up sooner or later.

Why, oh why, did it have to be now?

"I'm going to give that man a piece of my mind," a voice echoed through the door.

"Which man is that?" Snuock asked in a bland, almost incurious voice.

The footsteps stopped abruptly, then a silhouette filled the doorway.

It was Dory Jerritt, Jo and Mickey's mother. She was short and stocky with steel-gray hair in a practical, short cut. She looked like she could beat up a sailor with his own belaying pin, and would, too, if he gave her any attitude. As she stepped into the back room, her eyes picked up on the fluorescent lights overhead and seemed to glow with an eerie light.

"Alexander," she said.

"Why, as I live and breathe, if it isn't Dory Jerritt," Snuock said. "I should have expected that the locals would start arriving early this morning for gossip and gooseberry jam."

He looked like the cat that had got the cream. If he hadn't started out with the intent to damage the Jerritts with his raise in rent, it was definitely a side bonus.

"What have you done?" Dory asked.

"Nothing unreasonable," Snuock answered.

"You're going to drive my children out of business."

He tilted his head. "That's a shame...but if your children can't manage a business well enough to deal with fair market rental rates, then maybe they shouldn't be in the business. Of course, I'm always willing to discuss a loan...or a change of ownership. I could keep them hired on, doing what they love," he waved the pastry in his hand, then took another bite of it and swallowed it down with some coffee, "without having to worry their pretty little heads about all the paperwork. Tell them to think about it."

For a moment, Dory Jerritt was too flabbergasted for words. Her face turned such a bright, burning red that Angie began to worry that she would have a heart attack.

"You!"

"I'll leave the two of you alone to discuss matters," Snuock said. "Ms. Prouty? I trust that you'll provide Ms. Jerritt with your usual level-headed advice, and that you'll deliver my books as soon as possible, hmmm?"

He walked straight toward Dory, waited one long, tense moment while she stood in place, her fists clenched, then stepped out of his way. A second later he was gone.

Dory turned around and watched him. A car door slammed, an engine started, and car tires rolled over the gravel and out of the parking lot.

Angie brought Dory a cup of coffee, black—the way Dory liked it. She sipped at it slowly; it was too hot to gulp.

When about half the coffee had disappeared, Angie had gone through the mail and was starting to work on opening the boxes.

"It's not my children he's after," Dory said.

"Oh?" Angie hadn't realized that Snuock was *after* anyone—she'd only thought he was being his usual greedy self.

"It's Raymond Quinn."

Angie let out a breath. Alexander Snuock had bought the docks the previous year. He and Raymond Quinn had grown up on the island together—gone to school together. Both of them were sixty-five years old, and time hadn't softened their attitude toward each other. Quinn resented Snuock for his money; Snuock hated Quinn for his disrespect.

Quinn was a fisherman who rented one of Snuock's new docks. And his dock fees would be going up, too...a lot, probably.

"You're right," Angie said. "It makes perfect sense. That's what this is about. Mr. Snuock is trying to get rid of Raymond Quinn once and for all. As soon as he does, the rents will go back down."

Then she shook her head at the same time Dory did. Both of them knew that Snuock wasn't the type to let a trimmed dime go, let alone what had to be at least tens of thousands of dollars in extra rent every month—a drop in the bucket for Snuock, but one that he was too much of a miser not to try to sop up like a sponge.

"What am I saying?" Angie said. "This is permanent."

"At least we have until the end of the month to do something about this," Dory said.

"Like what?"

"I don't know. Something."

The rest of the morning, ironically, rambled along as normal. Angie drank her first cup of coffee and flipped through the mail again, almost out of habit. It wasn't like she hadn't planned for the slings and arrows of misfortune, but she hadn't budgeted for them to be quite so permanent. Her mind tumbled over itself, looking for a loophole, but couldn't find one: most of her profits were going to be wiped out for a while. She was going to have to raise her prices—never mind that she already struggled to deliver a service good enough for her customers to resist online book retailers—or else she was just going to have to find some other way to drive business. She *was* selling a few books online here and there, mostly from local authors. Should she host more book signings? Start her own small press, printing up more books on local history?

Pastries & Page-Turners had been open for three years now, and it was turning a profit, which was no mean achievement in this day and age of Internet sales. But what if that changed? What if she started losing money, what if...?

As customers wandered in and out of the store, they received her politest attention, although perhaps not her *fullest*. Distracted. That was the word for it.

One of them wanted a copy of a famous fiction book about submarines for her husband—but it couldn't possibly be *The Hunt for Red October* or anything by Clive Cussler, no; another one wanted a book, surely Angie knew which one, whose cover was in blue? A third wanted a book on local history; Angie steered him toward a small display where Nantucket history proudly faced the world, relieved that she could finally identify the right book. The submarine customer proudly brought *The Hunt for Red October* to the counter for Angie to ring up, saying that *she* had found it, even though Angie couldn't. The one who had wanted the book with the blue cover left with the first three books in the *Anne of Green Gables* series—none of which were especially blue.

Then, at ten a.m., Aunt Margery came in.

She was sixty-five years old, a white-haired beauty with black eyebrows and a perpetually catty, mischievous expression. The breeze had picked up, and was tugging the scarf she had tied around her head. Despite the blue sky, she wore a rain jacket. She leaned her bicycle up against the opposite side of the front door. When she came in the door, she made kissing noises and scratched Captain Parfait thoroughly, making him stand up, arch his back, and purr loudly. There was no question as to whom Captain Parfait *really* belonged. He butted her hand for more petting and gave an annoyed yowl when Aunt Margery clucked her tongue and walked through the store to the counter.

Angie got up and stretched.

"Hello, Aunt Margery."

"My dear." Aunt Margery, smelling strongly of face powder, gave Angie a hug and a kiss on each cheek. "I'm so glad to see you, even on such a terrible day as this. Have you heard the news?"

"About the raise in rent? Jo told me when she delivered the pastries."

Aunt Margery clucked her tongue. "It's a crime, that's what it is."

"It's unfair and infuriating, but I wouldn't call it a crime."

"You'll see. He's trying to drive Quinn out of business. He's having money problems, obviously. Quinn's been letting the condition of the boat go. He's on the edge of going under, financially. Mark my words, as soon as Quinn is out of business—"

"Rents will go back down? It's a nice thought, Aunt Margery, but I doubt that will happen."

"*So* cynical," Aunt Margery said. "Dory says that the bakery will have trouble, too. At least Ruth will be fine. She's a sharp one, Ruth." Aunt Margery shook her head admiringly. "I don't know *how*, but she'll manage to come out on top of this. Mark my words."

"Jo said that she and Mickey will be fine. They'll just have to sell more."

Angie wasn't in the habit of playing stupid with Aunt Margery, but sometimes she couldn't help herself. She decided not to bring up the fact that Jo hadn't been her only visitor that morning.

"Sell *more*?" Aunt Margery said. "Agatha Mary Clarissa Christie Prouty, you know very well that those two children couldn't work harder if their livelihoods depended on it. Which they do."

"Necessity is the mother of invention," Angie said. She hated being reminded of her full name; it was too cute for words, and she knew that her great-aunt was only doing it to bait her.

"'Invention, in my opinion, arises directly from idleness, possibly also from laziness. To save oneself trouble.'"

It was an Agatha Christie quote, from her autobiography, which Aunt Margery seemed to have memorized by heart.

She added, "I don't see how those children can be expected to invent *anything* at the pace they're going. Driven, yes. Sustainable, no."

"They'll figure something out," Angie said.

"Speak of the devil," Aunt Margery murmured.

A tall shape topped by a blaze of bobbing blond hair loped past the window and appeared at the doorway: Mickey Jerritt, Jo's twin. Even aside from Jo's choice in hair colors, the two could hardly look less alike. Mickey Jerritt had been made to be a professional basketball player and he would have been, too—MVP three consecutive years of high school, the highest scorer on the team, he took them to the state championships, college scouts circled him like vultures—until senior year when he landed on his ankle and shattered it. The whole town prayed it would heal, and it did, but imperfectly. And then to everyone's amazement, except perhaps his mother's, he had a love of baked goods, and not just eating them; he channeled all his grief into a mixing bowl—flour, sugar, butter, vanilla—the unlikely hero of high-school Home Ec. It was almost something to laugh at, if only it didn't make everyone want to cry so hard, too.

Angie waved at him. They'd dated during that tumultuous senior year. Mickey was sweet, not arrogant like you'd expect from a high school all star (even a fallen one); but blueberry muffins and pastries only offered so much solace, and when he couldn't realize his own dream, he turned his focus on Angie's. Set to be salutatorian of their class, she didn't need her boyfriend, of all people, telling her what to do to get into Brown, or Princeton, or Harvard, and how she was falling short. Her eighteen-year old self tried to understand what he was going through, but when he told her to stop reading so much, because it distracted her from schoolwork and college applications, she knew their love was not meant to be.

Now they were friends, if for no other reason than because it would have been more awkward not to be, but also because Mickey had his hands full keeping his business above water that he wasn't constantly trying to fix her. He had the kind of restless mind that never slowed down.

He entered the bookstore, ducking under the lintel and shaking his head. "Did you hear the news?"

"Jo told me," Angie said.

"It's terrible. Hello, Aunt Margery. Have you had breakfast? Would you like me to bring you up something from the bakery?"

Aunt Margery fought to keep a straight face. "I'm fine, dear."

"Just terrible," Mickey repeated, looking around the bookstore. His eye fixed on the well-lit pastry case; he took a corner of his white apron and wiped a fingerprint off the glass. "Some of those pastries aren't the best looking. I could bring some that look better."

"These are good," Angie said.

"It's no problem."

"I know...but you have a lot of work to do. Tell you what, if I get low, I'll come over and pick some out."

"Okay. I'll hold the good ones back for you." At six feet, five inches, his earnestness was disarming. It practically made Angie blush. "I won't lie, Angie, things are going to be tight. If only Snuock weren't such a miser. At least then I'd know that my money was out having fun. As it is, it's going to get bored. Nothing to do, sitting in a bank like that."

Angie smiled. "I'm sure that eventually it'll go out and have adventures."

"Yes, but I was planning to go spelunking in Chile in January. What kind of adventures is Snuock going to take it on? Subprime mortgage investments? I feel like this is all some kind of game to him—who can I make grovel? Dance, slave! Dance!"

Fortunately, the only two customers were at the back of the store, chatting flirtatiously with each other—it probably would have taken a gun going off to distract them.

"Mickey..."

"I know, I know. Business hours. I just needed to rant to someone who wasn't going to encourage me. Jo just eggs me on. 'I could just kill the guy!' and all that."

Angie shook her head. "If you're coming to *me* as the voice of sanity, you're seriously low on sanity."

"Nah. I don't think so." He winked at her and combed his fingers through his hair. "Don't forget, come and see me if you need more pastries. I want to make sure the good ones go to good homes. Stomachs, that is."

"I will."

"All right then, see you later."

Back out the door he went, hitting his forehead on the lintel. Fortunately for him, enough people had hit their heads there that Angie had fastened a foam bumper to it. Some of the buildings around here had been around long enough that the doors were smaller than most people were used to.

Aunt Margery was shaking her head. "That boy. He's been like that since he was born. Can't slow down...and can't shut up."

"It's kind of endearing, don't you think?"

Aunt Margery raised her eyebrows.

Angie cracked her neck, checked the coffee, poured herself a cup, and said, "I'm going to finish sorting the delivery books for this afternoon. Will you be all right up here?"

"Certainly."

Aunt Margery was looking out the front windows; one of her friends, Ruth Hepsabeth (who was also the owner of the antique shop next door) was passing by. Aunt Margery walked over to the front door and greeted her friend affectionately. The two of them chatted companionably just inside. Ruth wore a Bohemian-style skirt with a large, flowing blouse and about a dozen necklaces. She always looked like some sort of fortune-teller or New Age witch, but was sharp as a tack when it came to selling things on the Internet. Angie had gone to her for advice before.

"Quinn? Oh, he's in an *absolute* fury," Ruth was saying.

Aunt Margery smiled a wicked little grin. Captain Parfait stood up, stretched, then hopped off his shelf by the window to curl around Ruth's ankles. His tail curled like a question mark. Ruth bent over and picked up the cat, cuddling him into one arm as she scratched his ears and under his chin. The worse the gossip, the more Captain Parfait seemed to crave petting and affection from the gossipers—and Ruth Hepsabeth was a *terrible* gossip.

The two flirting lovebirds at the back of the store were still deep in conversation, pulling books off bookshelves and handing them to each other; they both had a sizable stack next to them on one of the small tables Angie had scattered throughout the store for such an occasion. It might be hours before they noticed there was nobody at the till…

Angie stepped into the stockroom, leaving the door cracked open, just in case. After opening the third of her book boxes, she made a face: Snuock's books had come in, and she was going to have to deliver them, or risk her rent going up even further.

Who knew what level Snuock might stoop to if he didn't get his books?

Chapter 2

SPECIAL DELIVERY

The road out to Alexander Snuock's mansion was a long and winding one, about five miles from the bookstore, just off Polpis Road. The last stretch was one of the few hills on Nantucket—and of course she always had to pedal it with a basket full of books! But the ride was a beautiful one, most of it on a well-maintained bike path, away from cars. On rainy or winter days, she would take her small VW Golf out onto the roads, but for the most part she preferred to ride. Even on days like today with a half-dozen heavy deliveries to make, people to chat with, dogs to admire, and orders to take.

Today, however, she found her legs pedaling slower and slower as she approached her final destination.

She still wanted to give Snuock a piece of her mind...but knew that wouldn't be wise.

Finally, she turned off Polpis Road and onto the driveway leading to Snuock Hill and the house that everyone on the island called "Snuock Manor." She stood up on the pedals and forced the bike forward, whether it wanted to or not.

She couldn't afford to lose Snuock as a client, let alone as a landlord. She could be civil. She could be courteous. She could be...

In what seemed like a split second, she had passed through the gatehouse and was at the front door of Snuock Manor, an enormous shake-sided building that sprawled around a long, circular loop of driveway. Discreetly tucked around the back of the house were lines of trees, a caretaker's lodge (complete with a barn), several guest cottages, and a horse paddock that was carefully mowed, but completely absent of horses. The back of the house opened onto the smaller Polpis harbor, overlooking waves, sky, and sailboats scudding around like birds.

Alexander Snuock's maid, Valerie, opened the door for her.

"Hello, Ms. Prouty. Mr. Snuock is expecting you. If you'll follow me?"

The two of them weren't friends, but Valerie usually wasn't as formal as this. Then again, Angie didn't usually deliver books on days in which a significant portion of the business owners on Nantucket Island had received large rent increases. The day might have been a bit tense around the mansion.

The inside of the house was light and airy, and caught the breeze off the water. The long curtains across some of the windows danced in graceful arcs. Valerie led Angie through the front room—a gigantic parlor overlooked by a wide balcony—and up a curving set of stairs that led to Snuock's study, a pale yellow room with white trim, decorated with oil paintings of boats sitting low in flat, almost unrippled water. His desk was under a small cupola roof; each hexagonal wall in the cupola had its own window, all facing the harbor. A model sailboat sat on the row of cupboards along the lower half of the wall. Underneath it was an antique silver pistol, very rococo...Angie clucked her tongue. No doubt it was a purchase made to accentuate the future display of his new books.

Alexander Snuock sat behind the desk, going over some paperwork.

He wasn't the kind of man to sit around and do nothing, even though he could afford that luxury—he could literally fill a bathtub with gold coins and do nothing for the rest of his life.

As usual, he smiled when he saw her.

He had a pleasant sort of face, with laugh lines around the eyes, thinning gray hair that was so smooth it looked like silk as it lay delicately on top of his head, and rounded shoulders. He had eyebrows so pale that they disappeared into his skin, and dimples on his cheeks.

He *looked* like a nice guy. That was the problem. But the pleasant look on his face could vanish in an instant. He could frown and make Angie quake in her sneakers. He could wink and make you feel repulsed—or charmed. It was an actor's face. It made you want to keep him happy, just so you didn't have to get an eyeful of his bad side.

"Ms. Prouty. You've brought my books, yes?"

"I have." Blue skies or no blue skies, she wrapped up all her customers' purchases in several layers, both to keep the purchases discreet and to protect them from the elements. She hadn't grown up on the island for nothing, to trust the weather to stay the same from one minute to the next.

Snuock could easily have afforded to purchase his books online; he could just as easily have afforded to purchase her entire store. What he *liked*, though, was having people wait on him hand and foot, using their time and expertise and attention. Putting them in positions where they owed him favors.

She had known, long before Aunt Margery had warned her, to treat Alexander Snuock with kid gloves. She had grown up around here, after all—and Alexander Snuock's father had been just as tyrannical as his son.

She shook her head: time to focus, not woolgather. Snuock cleared a place on his desk, and she lay the package on top of it. It was tied with heavy string, and the outer layer was heavy plastic. Snuock took out a gold paper knife, cut the string, and opened the package along the taped edges. As he unwrapped it, he handed each piece to Angie, who folded it neatly and set it on the countertop next to her.

Finally the stack of books was revealed. Snuock glanced at the titles and beamed at her. "These look delightful."

This time, he had asked her for at least four books on the history of Russia before World War I and the Communist Revolution—the time of Peter and Catherine the Great, and Ivan the Terrible. He had a taste for histories by historians with a dry sense of humor, and was a voracious reader; the stack of books she had brought him would occupy him for a week or two, but not much more. He tended to avoid novels; they passed by too quickly for him to get truly involved in them, he claimed.

He picked up the book at the top of the stack—*The Romanovs, 1613-1918*, by Simon Sebang Montefiore, and flipped it to a random page. "'When she went looking, she surprised Korsakov *in flagrante delicto* with Countess Bruce. In the resulting uproar, Korsakov had the impertinence to boast of his sexual antics with both women while demanding munificent gifts...Korsakov's affair ruined Catherine's friendship with Countess Bruce.' I should say it did. Did you notice my little purchase? One of a pair of presentation pistols from 1809, from Alexander I to...I don't remember. One of the Zubovs? At any rate, thank you for bringing these to me so soon, it has been a most trying day."

Angie's mouth fell open. Had the man completely forgotten that she was one of the business owners who was being heavily affected by his "trying day"?

"I'm sure it has been," she said. "What with so many of your tenants coming to you to complain of their sudden increase in tribute."

Rent. She had meant to say *rent.* But it was so hard to stay sane and tactful when one was within arm's reach of the Russians.

Snuock's faint eyebrows popped upward.

"It's been a trying day for all of us."

He squinted at her. "If I remember correctly, you came here from the McCory and Hiddle investment firm in Manhattan, as one of their more intelligent and savvy analysts. Oh, yes," he smiled at her surprised response. "I remember checking up on you when you applied for the lease on the shop. The previous owner of the store had gone out of business due to several unsound business practices, and I wanted to make sure that the literary community on the island would be supported by someone who wasn't such a...flake. You know how I feel about books. I wanted someone solid, and you *are* that."

When she didn't answer—what could she say? —he continued: "I repeat that I have no doubt that you, Ms. Prouty, aren't in the least bit of danger of losing your business. You have consistently kept expenses low, goodwill high, and provided what feels like an irreplaceable service to those of us who want to be kept in the books we love without the bother of having to look for them. *You* aren't in any danger."

"So this *is* about getting rid of Raymond Quinn," she said.

A sly smirk spread alongside half of his face. "Rumors do fly."

"But the bakery?" she asked.

"What about it?"

She didn't answer.

He looked down at his book, flipped a page back and forth, then said, without looking up, "Even if they're too proud to have anything to do with me, the Nantucket Bakery could easily be supported by the mother of the current owners, if they find themselves in trouble that they can't handle on their own, and you know it."

"But they are too proud."

Snuock grimaced. "As absurd as that sounds, I know how it is. The old families...we *are* proud, you know."

Both the Snuocks and the Proutys had been on the island for two hundred years or more—so had the Jerritts and the Earles, which were Jo and Mickey's mother's side of the family. Which family he was referring to, Angie had no idea.

"Can't you take it easy on them?"

"That would hardly be fair, would it? Now, if they were willing to do me some favors, I might find it worth my time to work out a reduction in rent."

"What kind of favors?"

"Tell them that if they're willing to swallow their pride, I'm sure we can come up with something."

Angie felt her face getting red. "And if I were to do you favors?"

Snuock's sly smile broadened as he looked down at his stack of books. "Aren't you already doing me a favor?"

Suddenly the time that Angie had spent searching for just the right collection of perfect books for her landlord felt sullied—almost dirty. She found herself making a face.

"Don't worry," Snuock said, ringing a small bell. "I won't ask anything of either of them that I wouldn't ask of you, ethically speaking. A catered event or two...it might be advantageous in more ways than one. You know I praise you to the moon to all my visitors from the City? 'You simply must stop by Pastries and Page-Turners. You know that the owner used to work with old Hiddle in

Manhattan? Really, she has a brilliance for picking out the perfect book..."

He stopped at the look on Angie's face and chuckled. He called out for Valerie.

Valerie stepped into the room. "Yes, Mr. Snuock?"

"Please offer Ms. Prouty any refreshments she would like, like many of our other visitors today, she has had a trying day. Once she's gone, you may see yourself out until...let's say, Saturday morning? I won't require any additional assistance—although if I do, I trust that I will find you at the caretaker's lodge?"

In a choked voice, Valerie said, "Yes, sir."

Angie forced herself not to clench her jaw or her fists and said, "Have a good afternoon, Mr. Snuock."

"I will leave a message with my next topic of research with you soon. Have a pleasant holiday."

In the distance, a line of white fire cut across the bright blue sky over the harbor, ending in a loud crack as a rocket exploded and clearly startled Snuock. A faint line of smoke hung in the air like a jet contrail.

"I would just as soon prefer it if they would leave off firing those infernal fireworks, they're nothing but a distraction."

"Indeed," Angie said. She turned her back on Snuock and followed Valerie out of the room.

Whatever Snuock had said to Valerie had left her in as much of a fury as Angie was in, if not more. It had seemed so innocuous, but that was Snuock's *modus operandi:* to get away with the most subtly painful insults, to find the secret hurts, and exploit them.

Angie *knew* that she was better off here, on Nantucket, away from the savage world of investment and finance. She didn't have the ruthless heart that was needed to survive—even if all she was doing was analysis, not hustling the actual deals.

But at this moment, it didn't seem to matter. Suddenly she felt small, like she'd been too incompetent to be a success, and that coming back here to her childhood home had been a mark of failure.

She and Valerie walked to the kitchen, with its acres of stainless-steel countertops. This wasn't one of those kitchens where the hostess puts the finishing touches on the dishes for her dinner guests as they arrive—this was the kind of kitchen where a battalion of white-coated young people filled up their silver trays with canapés while cooks frantically built seven-course meals for a hundred people.

"Bottle of water, Ms. Prouty?" Valerie asked.

Another rocket went screaming over the house and exploded in a loud crack.

"About a half-dozen cosmos would be nice," Angie muttered to herself.

Valerie grinned at her. "He does get under your skin, doesn't he?" She opened the restaurant-sized refrigerator and pulled out a pair of water bottles. She handed one to Angie and opened the other. "Here's to all the fireworks in the world," she said. "May they be fired often and late tonight."

It was still broad daylight. The noise and flashing lights after sunset would be far worse.

Angie touched the neck of her bottle to the side of Valerie's. "I'll drink to that."

Chapter 3

FOOT-IN-MOUTH DISEASE

Pastries & Page-Turners was keeping its doors open late on the third to catch the "fair trade winds" brought to the island by the tourists. Most of downtown was following suit. In the morning—Friday—the local businesses would all close up their shops and set up booths all along Main Street like fishermen casting out their nets.

It was supposed to be a gorgeous day tomorrow, in the upper seventies, breezy, and a five percent chance of rain. Angie had rented a small trailer and had packed it to the gills already; she had thought long and hard about the issue of moving books back and forth along the streets two years ago, and had worked out an efficient system: the trailer had a ramp along the back; the books were packed in special wheeled crates that she'd had built. Each crate was basically two solid-backed pine bookshelves facing each other. She fronted each shelf with foam padding to hold the books in place, pushed the bookshelves together facing each other, then latched them shut. They fit perfectly into a five-by-eight cargo trailer, and when it was time to pack up, all she had to do was fit the foam rubber back into place, close up the shelves, and wheel them back onto the trailer.

Admittedly, she had to put her back into it, especially if she hadn't sold that many books. But it was a good system, and she was starting to think about the possibility of marketing the travel shelves to other booksellers, flea markets, and other popup-type retailers.

She focused on her plans for tomorrow, going over the various ways she might improve her setup, trying to leave her conversation with Snuock behind her.

Still, she grinned every time she heard fireworks go off.

Soon she was back at the bookstore; she sent Aunt Margery off for supper—she said she was going over to Dory Jerritt's house for a few hours—and settled behind the counter with a Coronation chicken salad sandwich that Jo had brought over. The curry was mild and the currants were plentiful, just the way Angie liked it.

The afternoon stretched out into the evening, and the tourists came in and out of the shop, some of them browsers, others clearly book hounds—a few of them had brought notebooks with them that they consulted as they checked the shelves. *Those* ones Angie made a point of greeting personally, handing over her card, offering to make a search for missing volumes in series, favorite authors, signed copies, and listened to one of them tell a story of a notebook in Russian found in a grandparent's attic—one with a signed photograph of Czar Nicholas the Second. (Angie believed the photo existed, but doubted the signature; she almost asked the customer if she could take a look at the notebook if it was for sale—then shut her yap when she remembered that she wasn't presently doing favors for Alexander Snuock and his current interest in the Romanovs.) The hours stretched on, not exactly dull, but nevertheless almost hypnotizing her into forgetting how annoyed she was at Snuock, and how worried she was about the bakery.

What would she have been doing, if she'd stayed in Manhattan?

Getting ready for a night out at one of the most fashionable restaurants in the area, putting in a pair of diamond studs and adjusting her little black dress to show off her cleavage, smiling fondly at her ex, Doug McConnell—whether the smile was a genuine one or a false grimace would have depended on whether she'd already found out that he was a) cheating on her and b) passing off her work as his own stellar investment insights.

People had overlooked Angie because she was the girlfriend of a high-profile investment guru, and so they assumed he was the one with all the talent, when really he was just flashy and brash, and had duped everyone into believing he was a genius. It was Angie who had the talent, who understood decorum, and consequently would listen to people talk admiringly, usually at great length, about Doug, while she fantasized about the best murder methods to use at a ritzy restaurant, inside a cab, or at a cocktail party...

Someday, she promised herself, she would write one of those stories. Just to amuse herself and Aunt Margery, if nothing else.

The door opened and a tall, good-looking, blue-eyed guy in jeans and a wrinkled button-up waltzed in, bringing the smell of musk and sea with him as he passed by the sales counter and smiled at her. She felt as if she'd been hit with a jolt of electricity. She watched him as he gave the case with its last few pastries a glance then moved toward the fiction shelves.

He skimmed through the fiction quickly, then went deeper into the nonfiction shelves.

To her delight, he pulled out his wallet, took a piece of paper from it, and started using it to consult the shelves. A *serious* reader. She would definitely have to check in with him later to see if she could be of help.

She started with a pass of the bookstore, checking in with customers as she went. As she finally approached the man, she could almost hear the theme from "Jaws" in the background. Get control of yourself, she thought. But it wasn't that often that her "serious" readers were so completely hunky and cute.

"Finding everything?" she asked, in the coolest voice she could muster.

He looked at her and there was that smile again. "I'm looking for some books."

"Any luck?"

For a moment, he didn't answer, his eyes lingered on her face until he became self-conscious, and then gave a little jump and looked behind him. "I had some books...they were on a little table, right here—"

He waved a hand toward a place where there clearly *was* no table.

"I...seem to be slightly turned around in here," he said.

She fought back a grin. "What books were they?"

"A couple of things on the Russians."

She stepped into the aisle and spotted them right away: "Here you are."

"You must think I'm an idiot."

"Just easily distracted," she said. "Would you like me to keep these at the counter?"

"Please. If you don't mind."

"It's no problem." She picked up the stack of books. It was almost the same set that she'd packaged up and delivered to Alexander Snuock earlier in the day. When she went to the work of finding good books for her customers, she tended to order several copies, since she knew them well enough to recommend them by that point.

"You're missing one," she said.

"Oh?"

She found a copy of *Catherine the Great: Portrait of a Woman* by Robert K. Massie for him—someone had reshelved it badly, but the spine jumped out at her and she spotted it quickly—then held it out for him.

He chuckled. "That looks great. Just add it to the stack."

"I had a similar request last week," she said, a little awkwardly. When that grin spread across his face, he was positively enchanting. Dimples.

She shook her head and tried to stop drooling. "Let me know if you have any questions."

Time to abandon ship and head back to the counter, where she could pull herself an espresso and, hopefully, pull herself together, too.

"Will do," he said. She could feel his eye on her as she turned and walked away.

She lay the stack of books on one of the shelves behind the counter and took a deep breath. When she looked around the bookstore to see where her customers had gone off to, she noticed that one of them was standing right in front of her, waiting to check out. Oops.

She rang him up—an older gentleman with a stack of World War II histories who signed up for her mailing list—then found herself facing another customer, and another...

It was almost time to close up: the fireworks had been going off with increasing frequency as the evening began to settle down into actual darkness.

Finally, she looked up to see the Mr. Tall and Handsome, the last one in line. He had his hands in his pockets: he'd stayed almost another half-hour, but hadn't picked up a single additional book.

Almost as though he were waiting for her.

She glanced around the store; she'd have to double-check, but it seemed as though he was her last customer.

"Hello," he said. "May I have my Russians now?"

"I'm sorry," she said, blushing because she just couldn't help herself. "I didn't mean to keep you waiting."

"Not at all."

"I'm about to close up. Would you like a pastry or some coffee? Espresso?"

"Actually…" he hesitated. "Are you busy tonight? I'd like to get dinner and would love your company."

She tried not to swoon. He wanted *her* company.

He continued, "I mean, we could talk about books at least and who knows what else."

"I'd like that," she said. "I have some things to finish up here before I can leave, though. About, oh, fifteen minutes."

She had planned to stay at least an hour to make sure that everything was perfect for tomorrow, but, for Mr. Tall and Handsome, she could strip her plans down to the bare necessities and come in a little early in the morning.

He smiled and there were the dimples. Once again she felt a little hot in the face and a little weak in the knees.

"Any recommendations?" he asked. "I'll call and set up a reservation, make sure they're not closed or anything."

She checked her watch. Nine o'clock. They could be at Sheldon's Shuckery by nine-thirty; tonight he was staying open until midnight and passing out sparklers to guests. Sheldon was a local character, and the Shuckery would definitely impress the guy with local flavor.

"How do you feel about oysters?"

"I wouldn't say no. I try to load up on lobster rolls while I'm out here."

"Then I have a great place for you." She gave him the name. He nodded and stepped outside, flipping the open sign to "Closed" before closing the door and dialing.

It was only as she watched him under the streetlight—while third-of-July rockets exploded across town and lit up his face—that she realized she hadn't asked his name.

He waited for her as she raced around the store, dumping out the old coffee, cleaning out the pastry case, running one last load of dishes, and turning out the lights. As she took out the trash, she saw Ruth at her back door, taking out her own trash, and stopped to drag the heavy bag out to the bin for her. A thousand times she congratulated herself on having the foresight to get all her books ready throughout the week—carefully pulling out duplicate bestsellers, beach reads, popular history books, lots of Nantucket local books, kids' books, and books for teenagers that went far beyond Scholastic. She'd barely even left holes on her shelves in the shop—she'd been letting herself build up a backlog of likely candidates for her shelves.

Ten minutes later, she was ready.

He eyeballed her much-abused bike, still sitting in front of the store. "It's close enough to walk...are you okay leaving your bike here?"

"You never know with all the tourists," she admitted.

She wheeled the bike inside the door and locked it inside. Captain Parfait, who had gone into hiding earlier in the day, when all the tourists were around, had come out to his shelf and was watching the fireworks going off overhead. It probably didn't hurt that the old kitty was slightly deaf.

She scratched him on the head and assured him that she would give him all the love in the world once the weekend was over. He butted her hand, then stretched and yawned, as if to say, *I have the situation under control, madame. No need to worry about a thing.*

"There's a cat in your window!"

"He's been in hiding all day," she said apologetically. "He considers his main job to be watching the store for mice, not hanging out with tourists. He likes the locals, though."

"Does he? Find mice?"

"This morning he found me two gray yarn bobbles from my bookmarks, which he tore to shreds and left in front of the door. Does that count?"

They walked down the block and turned toward the water.

"Are you here long?" she asked, then found her face getting warmer again as she realized that she probably didn't sound like she was simply making small talk.

"You don't recognize me, do you?" He stopped and turned towards her.

She stopped awkwardly and studied him, and felt a little disoriented. Somehow he knew her, which meant she must have also known him, but she didn't know that she knew him. And how could she forget someone like him? Who would ever forget a face or physique like his? Then she felt a chill, maybe this guy was a hustler and he was conning her. Although it was beyond her why, all she had was a bookstore that made a modest profit.

Then it clicked: the books he picked out, the profile of his face under the streetlight...a weight sank in her gut. "Walter Snuock?"

He smiled. But this time, instead of the broad grin, he looked sheepish. "Hello, Angie."

She hung her head: she hadn't recognized him. At all.

Walter Snuock had been one of her best friends—back when she was in sixth and seventh grade. He'd been a rangy boy with a mop of hair, cute, but she would never have been able to imagine him as the handsome man before her now. His parents had gotten a divorce, and his mother, Phyllis, had moved with him to Boston. She hadn't seen or heard from him since, other than a few updates that Aunt Margery had passed along to her.

"Why didn't you tell me who you were in the shop?"

"I thought maybe you'd recognize me, and then when you didn't, I was...well to be honest, I was nervous. I know what my dad's been up to with the rent and I thought...you know, guilt by association."

She couldn't deny that it was precisely for that reason she felt a pang of disappointment; however, she also knew it was a knee-jerk reaction and that Walter was not his father.

She did her best to shake it off. "So what are you doing back here?"

"My parents divorce. It sounds ridiculous since it was over a decade ago, but it's the never-ending story. I'm here to try to make some kind of peace between them, which seems like a waste of time at the moment."

"I'm sorry. That sounds intense."

"Yeah. Have you met my parents?" He laughed out loud and shook his head. "They're both kind of impossible. But let's not talk about them. I'm just relieved to see an old friend. You still look as adorable as you did in middle school."

She eyed him skeptically. She didn't remember herself as adorable with the gap between her front teeth (later fixed by braces), and a case of acne that took countless visits to the dermatologist to remedy. At best it was her awkward stage.

"You were adorable," he said, obviously attuned to the doubtful expression on her face. "And still are...Well, I mean you're more than adorable...you're..." he groaned. "Will you please stop looking at me like that? I am not a flatterer. I mean it."

She started to giggle. "You don't look so bad either," she said, a mischievous grin on her face. A sea salt breeze swished past them. She looped her arm around his elbow and started tugging him down the street toward the restaurant.

"Come on, we can be awkward over a couple of lobster rolls as well as we can in the middle of the street, and I'm hungry."

His stomach growled loudly. "I haven't eaten since lunch," he admitted. "I saw you in the bookstore and decided to wait."

#

Sheldon owned his own property, thank goodness, so there wasn't too much residual resentment when Walter Snuock appeared and asked for his reservation. Sheldon recognized him right away, embarrassing Angie even further, and welcomed him back to town.

Sheldon's Shuckery was one of those places that looked like tourist traps but, when you scratched the surface, just got better and better. For one thing, the food was good—excellent actually, better than most of the more expensive places on the island.

For another, the paraphernalia on the walls wasn't even remotely normal: instead of rope fishing nets, flags, glass fishing floats, stuffed swordfish, and other touristy decorations, the walls were lined with locked glass cases filled with old patent medicine bottles, autopsy kits, boat logs, scrimshaw, lobster traps, miniature sailboats in bottles, even an old whale skeleton wired together and hanging from the ceiling. Customers could even eat oysters sitting on benches in a ship's boat from the 1890s.

Mingled with all the whaling antiques were painted wooden signs shaped like oyster halves with *horrible* puns:

We Don't Shuck Around.

The Shuck Stops Here!

Sunday: Monster Shuck Rally!

Just Shuckle Down and Get 'Er Done!

Sheldon Table (that was his real last name; his family had been on the island for generations) was just as unique as his restaurant. He was short, bald, and had a grin like a frog's. His skin was sunburnt and leathery; his eyes were deep-set under a Cro-Magnon forehead. He was married to a tall, stunning French woman with deep black, silky eyes—Jeanette Table. She seemed elegant, at least until she opened her mouth. Her sense of humor was just as bad as Sheldon's —she usually called him "Sir la Tah-bluh," or *sur la table,* French for "on the table."

Angie gladly gave him a hug when she saw him.

"Angie!" Sheldon exclaimed. "You've brought Walter back to the fold, I see. Are you here permanently?"

"Just visiting," Walter said.

Sheldon winked broadly at him and grabbed the menus out of his maître d's hands. "I've got these two," he said. He winked again. Angie's face was starting to turn red again.

Sheldon led them to a table outside on the deck overlooking the water. As usual, once the sun set, *none* of the families with children were seated outside, and *all* of the couples and singles were. If a party looked big and noisy, they got a back room with the other noisy parties; they could all yell over each other for all Sheldon cared.

Angie ordered the lobster bisque, a half-dozen Wellfleets, and an order of hushpuppies. Walter ordered a lobster roll with fries. They both ended up with Cisco Brewers' saisons in fat tulip glasses. Sheldon brought them a dish of shrimp dip and house-made, thick potato chips.

Walter said, "So, what's happened to you since seventh grade? I'm not surprised that you're a bookseller, the way you were always reading even back then."

"When my parents moved to Florida—"

"What? Florida? But the weather is so terrible there!"

She laughed. "I know! But they've always been a little bit crazy. Let me back up. They stayed in one place—here, on Nantucket—until I graduated from high school, then announced that they had *never* had any patience for staying in one place for long, and the only reason they had was so I could grow up without having to switch schools a dozen times. Then they sold their house, bought a food truck, and started following a circus around."

"You're joking."

"Not at all. But finally, a couple of years ago, they announced that they were going to settle down in Florida. Mom said, 'There's enough crazy in one place to keep us busy for a while.'"

Walter shook his head. "Your mom always seemed so *normal*."

"I thought so, too. You know how some people's parents...uh..."

"Suddenly get divorced out of the blue?" he asked, raising one eyebrow.

"Yes. My parents suddenly got divorced from being normal. Just like that."

"I've never heard of that before."

"Aunt Margery said that it was pretty normal for our family. The Prouty's either wander early and come back, or stay and raise a family until they have kids of their own and then leave to travel the world. One or the other."

"And you?"

"I wandered early. I spent half my college in L.A., and the other half at Oxford."

"No!"

She dropped into R.P., the accent of kings: "We most assuredly did. We can be quite posh when we feel like it."

He laughed.

"Anyway, when I came back with a double B.A. in literature and statistics—"

"You always were a math whiz. How many times did I copy your homework?"

"That would be zero. You constantly begged me for it, but I would never let you because—"

"Because how was I ever going to learn anything if I didn't do the work?"

Now she had a sheepish smile. "You remember."

"How could I forget? I almost flunked out of Mr. Hall's class." He shook his head, clearly amused, and shoved a chip full of smoked shrimp dip into his mouth.

"Oh, I didn't know that. I would have tutored you had you asked. Why am I feeling guilty?"

"You shouldn't. I like a woman with standards."

Her faced must have pinged red because he started laughing. In a second she was going to break a sweat.

"So go on," he said. "What did you do after college?"

"I worked for a Manhattan investment firm for a while. I was pretty good at it and made our clients a lot of money...and managed to save up a good chunk myself. Then I found out my boyfriend was cheating on me, *and* claiming my analysis work for his own"

"He obviously didn't know you. You must have broken up with him right away."

She'd never seen herself so clearly. "I'm not sure which made me angrier him passing off my work as his own or the cheating."

"The former, definitely."

"Yeah. I think so." Now they were both laughing. "I got out of the relationship and Manhattan, came back home to Nantucket, moved in with Aunt Margery, and leased the bookstore when it came up."

When they finally took a breath, Angie noticed a sudden change in Walter's expression. He stared down at the chips in front of him. Angie suddenly got the feeling he was hiding something.

"What?" she asked.

"I'm trying to decide whether to tell you something."

"What is it? Have you been stalking me?" she joked.

"No, but my father might have been. He likes to keep track of locals who are doing well, in case he can hit them up for a favor...you know how he is by now, I'm sure."

"That's true," she said ruefully. "Your father definitely likes holding favors over people's heads."

"Well, he *might* have helped drive the previous bookstore owner out of business so that you could get the store you wanted."

She clucked her tongue. "After the conversation I had with him earlier today, I wouldn't be surprised. He isn't the most ethical person in the world. And he loves having a hold over people." Another piece of the puzzle dropped into place: "Is that why you're here? Because he called in a favor?"

"Got it in one." Walter said. "I'm here to get my mother to behave, If I don't get her to do what he wants, he's going to cut off my allowance." Walter sighed. "You'd think that after all these years he wouldn't care what mom did, but you know how he is, he craves the control."

Angie wanted to tell him that he obviously was smart enough not to need it, but she had no idea what Walter did for a living, so she bit back the comment. She chewed on a potato chip, trying to decide whether to ask him what was up with his mother, but decided not to. If he wanted to tell her about his life, that was one thing, but she didn't need to pry.

No doubt Aunt Margery was finding out the scoop from Dory, anyway.

"I wish you the best of luck sorting out that mess," she said, sincerely. If Snuock was a jerk to her, she could only imagine what being his son must be like.

The wait staff brought their food to the table, and they both started to eat. Sheldon appeared, beaming, to ask them how it was: "Eggshellent," Angie said.

"I still have dreams about your lobster rolls," Walter added. "When Mom and I used to come out here for lunch when she was getting her hair done."

"How is your mother?" Sheldon asked.

"Oh, she's been back on the island for a while," Walter said. "Just keeping to herself. But Dad..."

Sheldon shook his head and patted Walter's shoulder as if he were still a boy. "Don't worry, kid. Trust me on this one: you take after your mother."

"Thanks. I think."

It was true; Walter *didn't* take after his father—except when his grin burst out, and that was just a physical resemblance.

"I'll let you two kids eat. Enjoy!" Sheldon wandered off, stopping at tables to talk to the late-night guests out on the patio.

The night was clear and the stars were beautiful, if somewhat hazed over by a layer of mist mingled with gunpowder coming in off the harbor.

"It's going to be foggy in the morning," Walter said, as if he were saying something that surprised him. "I remember that. When it looks like this at night, it's going to be foggy in the morning."

"Enough about your father and my parents," Angie said. "Tell me what you did, after you left Nantucket."

"Well, first we went to Ohio..."

#

The evening ended with an escort back to the bookshop and a kiss on the cheek.

"This was lovely," Walter said.

Angie could only agree: it had been a beautiful night. She couldn't say that they'd caught up on old times, although Angie did tell him what had happened to a few of their classmates, including Jo and Mickey.

"They're going to lose the bakery, aren't they?" he said.

"I wouldn't go that far," she said. "But it's definitely going to be tight. Over seven hundred dollars a month."

She grimaced, wondering what fraction of his monthly allowance from his father that might be—but of course she didn't ask. She had found out that Walter owned some property in New Jersey and was working his way through a law degree, not because he wanted to be a lawyer, but because having a law degree gave him some authority. He was his father's only heir, and apparently he was taking it seriously. He even had a master's degree in business that he called "mostly worthless" and was using most of his allowance as venture capital in order to test his ideas; he spent a good deal of the meal picking Angie's brains about investment strategies and analysis—although she had to beg off, saying that she'd been out of the game for three years, and a lot had changed.

"But you're all right," he said. "Financially speaking, I mean."

"I should be."

Every time he brought it up, it irritated her. He seemed genuinely concerned about her, but it was like he didn't care about Jo and Mickey—even though they'd all gone from kindergarten through middle school together.

"I should let you go," he said. "I'm sure you need some sleep before you set up in the morning."

She did. She let herself yawn conspicuously before unlocking the bookshop door and wheeling her bike out.

"Are you sure you don't want a ride?" he asked.

"I'm fine."

Captain Parfait was no longer in the window; fortunately, there were no decapitated bookmarks in front of the door, either.

Walter stood by the door with his hands in his pockets; when she didn't invite him home—or whatever it was that he was expecting—he straightened up, said "Goodnight," and turned around and walked the opposite way down the street, turning off at the end of the next block, toward a public parking area. One thing she'd learned from her last relationship: take it slow. It takes time for a person to show their true colors. So even though her desire urged her to see where the night would take them, her wisdom told her to pack it up and go home.

She got on the bike and began pedaling back to her house. Soon she reached the tiny home that she shared with Aunt Margery; it had been in the family for generations, which was lucky—even as small as it was, Angie wouldn't have been able to afford it on her own. It was a tiny shake-sided cottage that had been built all the way back in 1835, but was well kept up. It had had a major renovation in 1927, and then again in 1974, and finally Angie's parents had redone the kitchen and bathrooms for her in 2005, also painting the front door bright blue. The doorways were narrow and low, the stairs to the upper floor more like a ladder than normal stairs, and the floors creaked constantly, even when nobody was walking on them. The wood inside the house glowed golden from almost two centuries of polish. All the furniture was antiques, even the light fixtures, floor grates, and window treatments. Of course everything was decorated in books, from a second edition OED (all twenty volumes) to the Agatha Christie Mystery Collection from Bantam (eighty-two volumes in black vinyl cloth over padded boards). Aunt Margery had a fascination with old clocks, too, even if she never bothered to set them to the same time. A soft purr of tick tocks filled the house. Everything smelled slightly of old books—granted, not as strongly as the actual bookstore, but still close.

Aunt Margery had beat Angie home; she was sitting in the front room in an overstuffed armchair that was decorated with a fabric print of cats lying on books. She was flipping through a photograph album, and barely looked up when Angie came in and kicked off her shoes by the door.

"How did it go?" she asked.

"How did what go?"

"Your date with Walter Snuock, of course," Aunt Margery said. She looked up and fluttered her eyelashes. "You don't think I didn't hear about *that* from Sheldon almost right away, did you?"

Angie laughed. "You don't miss a trick, do you?"

"I might, but my friends won't."

Angie shook a finger at her great-aunt. "Spies, I tell you. Spies."

"'From infancy on, we are all spies; the shame is not in this but that the secrets to be discovered are so paltry and so few.' Updike."

Angie snorted. "Are you trying to say that I should have done more than get a peck on the cheek? We *are* getting a nasty rent increase from his father."

"Maybe he'll put in a good word for the store."

"I doubt his father would listen to it. When I went up to the mansion to deliver his books, he mentioned that he was spending the rest of the night alone, which means that he *wasn't* spending time with his son."

"Or his ex-wife."

"I didn't know Phyllis had been back on the island."

"You don't know Phyllis, period. They left when you were in what...

sixth or seventh grade? At twelve or thirteen how much time did you ever spend talking to Phyllis Snuock?"

"All right, all right, but it's gossip related to the Snuocks. I would have thought that you'd have told me all about it."

"I don't tell you half of what's going on in this town. But how was the date?"

Angie sighed and sat in the overstuffed chair opposite her great-aunt. She'd been hoping to go up to bed without having to give her aunt the blow-by-blow. But of course Aunt Margery was one of the nosiest people she knew, and Angie wouldn't hear the end of it if she didn't come clean now.

Aunt Margery nodded thoughtfully through Angie's description of the afternoon and evening—then abruptly stood up, made a very showy yawn, and said that she was going to bed.

"But you haven't told me about your evening," Angie said.

"We have an early morning of it," Aunt Margery said, completely unfairly. "I'll tell you all about it tomorrow."

And then she yawned and retreated to the former ground-floor study that had been turned into her bedroom, "to save her knees," as she said, firmly closing the door behind her.

Angie blinked twice, totally disappointed by her aunt's unwillingness to share the gossip, then locked up and went upstairs to bed.

#

Late that night, she woke up out of a sound sleep. Had she heard a noise from downstairs? It was just after one a.m. The house itself was silent and still, but a breeze had picked up overnight, and she could hear the rush of it blowing in from the harbor. She tried to close her eyes and go back to sleep, but her subconscious took advantage of the fact that she was awake and started making to-do lists for the morning.

She promised her subconscious that she was ready, that everything would be fine, that she didn't need to get up and check on the trailer she'd rented to make sure that thieves hadn't broken into it and—because book thieves were the absolute worst—stolen all her books.

Her subconscious was having none of it. Thieves were breaking into her trailer, she'd forgotten to pack cash and receipts in her bag, and Captain Parfait was facing off against a giant rabid monster rat in the bookstore...

She threw back the covers and swung herself out of her antique bedstead. She could ignore the threat to Captain Parfait, but not to her book business. She would quickly check that the trailer or the house hadn't been broken into, and she would look to see if she had cash, card swiper, and paper receipts in the bag she always packed for sales days.

She padded down the stairs and felt her skin prickle.

What was the sound that had woken her, anyway?

The lights in the kitchen were on, and the back door was unlocked. Aunt Margery's shoes were missing from beside the door.

Angie took a quick look into her bedroom: the bed was empty. The covers had been laid upon but not pulled back; a paperback was lying face down on the other side of the bed. Angie tucked the bookmark on the bedside table between the pages: *Tinker, Tailor, Soldier, Spy* by John le Carré, one of Aunt Margery's favorite novels.

Angie slipped on a jacket and put on her shoes, her pajama shorts should be good enough for now.

The back of the trailer was still closed up tight, the lock gleaming in the moonlight.

Aunt Margery's car was still there, and both their bikes as well.

Where had she gone?

Angie closed her eyes and felt the breeze coming off the harbor, then started walking for the beach. A rocket went off in the distance, its explosion more of a crackle than a boom. A few voices echoed down the streets; the bars had closed, but a few late-nighters were still at it. The air tickled her throat—tomorrow it would sting from all the gunpowder in the air. The dogs had either settled down for the night or were hiding behind their owners' couches. A pair of headlights swerved toward her as a car turned onto the street, then away again.

The sound of the harbor breeze brushed gently along the streets, not hard enough to pick up dust, but fresh and cool and soothing. Angie took a set of cement stairs down toward the shore. The Brant Point Lighthouse flashed red in the dark to her left; a few of the docked boats had their lights on. As she came down the hill, she noticed that the *Woolgatherer*, Raymond Quinn's fishing boat, was missing from its slip.

A small bonfire was burning on the beach near one of the paddleboat shops. Angie zipped up her jacket so it wouldn't flap in the breeze, much stronger now. The crash of waves had replaced the sound of the breeze.

A single figure sat next to the small bonfire on the sand under the high-tide mark, legs stretched out forward with the toes turned out. By the silhouette against the fire, it was easy to see that it was Aunt Margery. As long as she didn't stay long enough to get swept away by the tide, she'd be all right. She'd been having a lot of sleepless nights lately, but then she always had—and about two or three times a year, she'd stay down by the water almost all night. When Angie had been young, her mother had mentioned it, and Angie had asked the reason why.

"I'm waiting for my pirate to come home," Aunt Margery had said.

"Didn't you know? I was once in love with a pirate who went out to sea and never came home, although sometimes he sends me bottles back from the ocean with messages."

"What kind of messages?" she'd asked, and Aunt Margery had told her an improbable tale of mermaids, gun battles, and forgotten grottos. The stories of Aunt Margery's unnamed pirate had continued for years, and Angie still remembered them fondly. Her great-aunt had never married, and Angie had never heard the reason why. Maybe it was half-true, and there was a lost love whom she thought about on those long, sleepless nights.

Half of her wanted to call down to her great-aunt and tell her to get to bed or she'd be tired the next day—but the other half stopped her and made her walk back home and go to bed. Who was Angie to complain if Aunt Margery needed to consult her pirate about her worries more than she needed sleep?

Chapter 4

A FESTIVE OCCASION

Pastries & Page-Turners was just far enough off the historic downtown main route that it made sense to set up a separate booth, one well stocked with fliers showing where the main bookstore was located. The morning fog was thick, but not impossible, the sun was already starting to burn it off. Boat horns echoed across the harbor.

Angie spread sunscreen on her arms and neck and face, then looked over her shelves: six-thirty a.m. and everything was ready, including her pots full of coffee and table full of pastries clearly marked as being from the bakery. Mickey had been waiting for her at the booth, shifting from foot to foot.

"Make sure you pull any ugly-looking ones and I'll replace them. I'll have Jo check on you at seven."

"I don't think I'll be sold out by then. Honestly, everyone's still asleep."

Most of the booths and tents hadn't been set up yet; technically, she didn't have to have everything ready to go before eight-thirty, but she had risen at five a.m. like a jack-in-the-box. The older she got, the more of a morning person she became...and if she was anxious about *anything*, she'd be awake at least an hour earlier than she needed to be.

"They'll smell the coffee," Mickey said. "The people who are here the earliest will be the locals and if I can impress the locals then boom! We'll have it made. Everyone will remember these pastries." He had to be more anxious than she was. She let him run on for a while, at least until he started pacing back and forth, and then she reminded him that he had his own booth to set up—at which point he strode off without even saying goodbye.

She giggled at his back, poured herself a cup of coffee, and pulled out a cheese Danish that didn't look *quite* as perfect as Mickey might have wanted.

It was like casting a spell. Within moments, three people were standing in front of her booth, wanting coffee before they had to set up, eyeballing her mobile bookshelves. "I wonder if I could get some like those to put my pottery on?" She handed out cards. Something could be arranged. "I'd owe you one..."

Favors. They made the small business world go 'round. Snuock had understood that and exploited it ruthlessly; she intended to be *far* more fair.

~

Soon the fog had burned off, the sun had come out, and the tourists and townies had emerged from their slumber. Festival food reigned along the streets: diets were dropped, flags were waved, and ice cream was consumed by the bucket. The streets were filled with a happy, contented air—a little restless with all the crowds of people moving along the street, but still pleasant. Captain Parfait would have hated the scene with a passion. All those moving legs. All those dogs on leashes. All those baby strollers. Horns echoed across the harbor. Gulls swooped in to collect the choice treats now available on the street. People fanned themselves with programs and fliers—it was warm, almost tending toward hot, now that the previous night's breeze had fallen mostly still. A few of the kids were already sparkling with red, white, and blue lights attached to baseball caps or worn as necklaces. Firecrackers echoed along the streets.

It was a good day.

She was selling books, passing out fliers, and providing refreshment for tired parents who would basically sell their souls for something that wasn't syrupy-sweet to drink. Her tent was a heavy one, and people lingered in the shade. Paperbacks were jumping off the shelves, hardbacks less so. Books were being purchased in ones or twos, not stacks—although if she'd had a bag sale for less-than-perfect used paperbacks, she probably could have done well with that, too.

Further down the aisle of booths, she saw Jo and Mickey at their tent, with a line of customers waiting on them. Dory Jerritt was with them at their booth most of the time, and usually ended up being the one who was sent to check up on Angie's pastry supplies.

"How's it going over there?" Angie asked. "Good sales?"

Dory, who looked exhausted, read between the lines and said, "They'll make up the extra cash next month at least." She shook her head. "After that? We'll just have to pray."

Everyone seemed to pass along the front of the tents in the middle of the street—Walter Snuock walked by several times, each time stopping to talk with Angie if she wasn't busy, or at least to smile, and once he even brought his mother with him. Raymond Quinn walked by, a bearded giant, beetle-browed and scowling, holding a huge tutti-frutti ice cream cone in one fist and a plastic goodie bag in the other. He couldn't possibly be as hateful as people described him—he licked his ice cream cone and winked at a pair of little babies in a stroller as they stared at him.

Aunt Margery was late and Angie's coffee supplies were getting low. It was almost noon—Angie was tempted to call and see if her great-aunt was all right, late night or not. Then someone touched Angie on her shoulder from behind—and there she was.

"Happy Fourth," Angie said. "And good morning, sunshine."

"You shouldn't have let me sleep in so late," Aunt Margery grumbled. She was wearing a lightweight button-up shirt over a tank top to help fend off the sun, and a pair of dark sunglasses.

"Waiting for your pirate captain again?" Angie asked.

Aunt Margery grunted. "You'd think I'd have figured out that he was never coming back by now. All those mermaids." She settled in behind the counter. "You're dancing from foot to foot, Agnes. Everything all right?"

"We're almost out of coffee," Angie admitted. The small coffee pots were all she had left—the big urns were empty and she had run out of water for brewing more. "I *was* about to call you."

"Go ahead and run and get some water. I'll keep things under control here. Do Mickey and Jo have any coffee left? I hate to impose on them for water, but..."

"Dory says they're out of decaf but also thinks that's no big loss."

"I'll send 'em over there, then, if we run out."

Angie gave her great-aunt a kiss on her cheek, surreptitiously checking for sunscreen, and smelled cocoa butter and coconut. All good. "Thank you."

Aunt Margery gave a short cough and said, "And there's Phyllis with Walter. I haven't seen *her* out in ages."

Angie looked around and spotted Walter; next to him was a taller woman with a face similar to his, about Aunt Margery's age, only oddly young looking. She was stooped, though, and her knuckles were slightly swollen. Her face might have escaped some of the ravages of time, but her joints hadn't, poor thing.

Walter glanced over, spotted her looking his way, and waved.

"Go on," Aunt Margery said, and Angie slipped through the crowd, dodging this way and that, until she was standing on one side of Walter, with his mother on the other.

"Angie, you remember my mom, Phyllis?" Walter said.

Angie said, "I'm sorry, Phyllis. Really I don't. It's been what? Fifteen years?

Phyllis nodded stiffly, without really greeting her. "I'm not a big reader."

Angie realized the woman was sort-of apologizing; she was explaining why she hadn't stopped in to see her. "Some people aren't," Angie said pleasantly. "Although if you ever *do* need a book, I'm sure I can find one or two that you'd like."

"I don't even watch television."

"Are you a knitter, then?" Angie had had similar conversations inside the bookstore with women who had followed their husbands in—with men, it was generally something having to do with models—model cars, model trains, model airplanes, model armies.

Phyllis's face lit up. The change wasn't as drastic as on her son's face, but it made Angie exhale with relief. "Yes! It shows, doesn't it?"

"Oh, just a lucky guess," Angie said.

Phyllis wasn't wearing a single knitted piece of clothing or accessory, and didn't have knitting needles in her hairdo or anything. Nevertheless, she patted Walter's hand as if to congratulate him for introducing her to someone so clever. Angie couldn't help smiling.

Then Phyllis's eyes caught something further down the busy street. Angie glanced behind her—she couldn't help it—but wasn't sure what Phyllis was looking at. Both she and Walter were taller than Angie was, and could see over the heads in the crowd.

Walter frowned in the same direction that his mother was looking.

Phyllis said, "I suppose I'll leave you two young people to it then, shall I? I'm going to have lunch with Denise, I think. I've had enough of the crowds today."

"Would you like me to walk you back to her house?" Walter asked.

"No, I think I'd rather have the time to clear my thoughts." She adjusted her quilted handbag; now that Angie was looking for it, she could see a skein of yarn through the open top. "Denise is an old friend, but she often has more gossip to pass along than I can stomach. Always winking and dropping hints."

"There *is* a lot of gossip in this town," Angie said.

Phyllis gave her a sharp look, but it softened after a split second. "And you don't mean the slightest thing by that, do you?"

"No?" Angie said. "I'm sorry, did I say something wrong?" If Phyllis was the subject of town gossip, Angie hadn't heard it yet, but now she was terribly curious.

Phyllis reached across Walter and patted her on the hand. "You're just like your mother. So vibrant. Only she was one of the Prouty go-ers and you're more one of the stay-ers. I'll make sure to come and visit you at your bookstore if I need a knitting book."

"I'll make sure we have some good ones on hand," Angie said, struggling a little to keep up. Phyllis's tone felt a little patronizing, but then again she'd been with Alexander Snuock for a over a decade. Maybe he had rubbed off on her a little.

Phyllis patted her hand again, then patted her son's arm and turned around, walking with surprising, long-legged swiftness into the crowd, not so much dodging around the other pedestrians as walking straight toward them and expecting them to get out of her way. She must not be suffering too badly from arthritis, Angie thought. In a moment she had reached the end of a block, passed around the car barriers, and disappeared.

"There you have her, my mother," Walter said. "Tall, awkward, random, and obliviously rude."

"So clearly she's your favorite parent," Angie joked. As soon as it was out of her mouth, she regretted saying it.

But Walter just laughed. "It's true, she is. Tell me, what would you like to do today?"

"Oh, I have to work," she said regretfully, maybe teasing him a little. "You know? At the bookstore booth?"

"Right. I was just hoping I could distract you for a moment or two." He put his hands in his pant pockets and shrugged, as if to say he had to at least try.

"Well, if you don't mind helping me run errands, we can take our time," she added. "Aunt Margery slept in late this morning, and I'm on a break for lunch and to refill the coffee urns. And you look like exactly the kind of strapping young man who could be bribed to help me carry heavy things."

"Bribed?" he asked hopefully.

"Bribed."

That was the only real downside to her excellent mobile bookselling system: she had yet to come up with a way to bring enough water for coffee to these things. It was like Hofstadter's law: *It always takes longer than you expect, even when you take into account Hofstadter's law.* Angie always needed more water for coffee than she expected, even when she took into account that she'd brought more water than last time. Of course it didn't help that she kept her prices low at these events—fifty cents a cup, fifty cents for cream or soy milk, and a big tip jar to collect change. She wasn't selling coffee; she was selling goodwill and advertising: her cups all had her bookstore logo on the side. The water she lugged around to do it never got any lighter, though.

"Then that's a plan," Walter said.

She took his arm and led him the same direction his mother had gone, turning away from the packed street downtown and walking swiftly back toward the shop.

While she was there, she checked the mail...and found another box of books. She opened it to see if they were ones that she should take with her to the booth—in case their readers showed up—and found three copies of another Russian book.

She'd forgotten about it, and so had Snuock, apparently. But the second he remembered there would be hell to pay. She'd better just deliver it later tonight.

"Anything good?" Walter asked.

She showed him a copy of the book, *Peter the Great: His Life and World*, by Robert Massie. "Want one?"

"Yes, please."

An hour later they started walking back, having eaten a picnic lunch, bribed one of the local teenagers to take twenty gallons of water in one-gallon jugs over to the bookstore booth, and generally talked about the important things in life: their favorite authors. Angie had been named after Agatha Christie, of course, but her favorite writer was currently M.C. Beaton, with Alan Bradley a close second. Oh, she had gone through phases earlier in her life where she had loved Virginia Woolf and James Joyce, but as she had eased up a bit on her ambitions to become rich so she could retire early (from a job she hated), her tastes in fiction had relaxed as well.

Walter's favorite authors were Erik Larson (here she nodded; she'd loved *The Devil in the White City* and *Thunderstruck*), Kurt Vonnegut, and Adam Hochschild. When she asked him what kind of popular fiction he read when he wasn't reading intense literary novels or intense history books, he grinned and said that intense was more to his taste than popular.

Oh, it was *on*. They argued pleasantly about literary versus popular fiction, never getting irritated with each other, conceding a few points here and there, and generally spending more time teasing each other than anything else.

Angie found herself hoping that he would stick around for a while, even after he'd resolved whatever was going on between his parents.

The rest of the afternoon and into the evening was pleasant, with the crowds staying steady throughout the day. Angie's cases would be much easier to push up the short ramp into the trailer from all the books she had sold. Occasionally, she'd made more money at the store—usually after coming across an underappreciated rare edition and selling it online to a collector—but she would still have to call the sales that day an unqualified success.

Aunt Margery was quiet and reserved with both Angie and the customers, which wasn't like her. She wasn't the most gregarious person in the world and tended to be much more open around people she knew—but at events like this, she usually put on a cheerful public face, the kind that could convince a stranger that she had never had an introverted day in her life.

At five thirty, she said, "My dear, I'm not feeling well. Would you mind if I went home for a bit?"

"Not at all," Angie said. "Take all the time you need. In fact, I can close up without you, if you need to lie down for a while."

Aunt Margery made a face. "I'm not feeling *that* poorly. I'm not old enough to be taking naps in the late afternoon. That's for old people."

"I'm old enough for naps in the late afternoon," Angie announced.

"You have no pride."

"Nope! But I do hope you feel better."

"Thank you." Aunt Margery worked her way out of the booth and back up the street. From behind, she looked defeated—her shoulders slumped, her head hung down, and her gait was slow and shuffling.

Angie had a flash of sudden worry: was Aunt Margery worried about something she didn't know about? Was she having more serious issues that she didn't want to talk about? Health issues?

She had seemed to come down with a very serious mood since she had had supper with Dory Jerritt last night. Of course Dory had to be worried about the bakery—but it seemed more than that.

Angie tried to shake off the feeling that some terrible event was hanging over the heads of the people she knew, just out of sight. She hoped it wasn't about money. Money was something that could generally be fixed, Business problems, too—with thought and support. But health problems and family problems, those could be swift and tragic. And Aunt Margery was exactly the kind of person who would try to spare Angie that kind of worry, at least until the festival was over.

~

That night, just before sunset, she had started packing everything up. Most of the festival goers had headed toward the harbor to get a better view of the fireworks; the few that were left were far more interested in the dregs of the coffee than they were in the books that they squinted at in the long shadows cast along the street.

She considered whether to set up lights for evening events—but mainly people didn't want to shop for books along the street at a festival in the evening, they wanted to eat and dance and watch fireworks and listen to music. So she shelved that idea for the time being and closed up the shelves, packing them with their foam-rubber pads and latching them shut. Aunt Margery hadn't returned; Angie would have to walk back to her trailer and drive it down here on her own, and hope that no one would abscond with her equipment.

Then Walter appeared. His eyes shone like bright jewels in his tanned face. "I'm here for my bribe," he said cheerfully.

He certainly was striking. She wished her feet didn't hurt, that she hadn't drunk so much coffee, and that she didn't need a shower as badly as she did. Food and socializing were the last things on her mind—but she was still glad to see him.

"I'll have to bribe you later," she said. "I have to get the books packed up, and I don't have Aunt Margery here to watch things while I go get the trailer."

"Oh!" he said. "I can watch it for a few minutes, if you need me to."

"Would you?"

In a flash she was off, walking as quickly as she could toward her car and the trailer. The side streets were still officially blocked off, but police officers were waving booth owners in to pack up their wares.

Angie spotted Mickey yawning behind the wheel of his SUV and waved at him, then drove slowly around the corner to her booth.

Walter was gone.

Angie sighed and parked the trailer in front of the bookshelves. It wasn't like he was an employee or anything; she couldn't expect him to hang around and do favors for her all the time. She got out of the car, opened the back of the trailer, pulled out the ramp, and walked over to the booth.

On the table where she'd been ringing up sales was a note. *Sorry, emergency phone call from Mom. I hope everything goes okay! And I'm so sorry—be back ASAP to see if you still need help.*

She sighed again. She couldn't even be annoyed now. Of course he'd rushed off to help his mother—he was just that sweet. She hoped it wasn't anything too serious.

She loaded the bookshelves into the trailer, took down the tent and booth, and loaded those, then dumped out the last of the coffee into the storm drain. She was half asleep on her feet.

Amateur fireworks had really started to go off. They had been going off all day, but now it was starting to get serious. She thought she could even hear the younger partiers over on the south beaches shooting them off, although with all the buildings around her, she couldn't see them.

She yawned and drove the trailer carefully back to the bookstore, leaving it parked in the back parking lot and checking the padlock a half-dozen times before she remembered that she needed to check on Captain Parfait again.

It was full dark by then, so he'd moved away from the window in order to stalk the mice that he was sure were threatening to damage her books, but he was happy to accept treats and pets. He head-butted her legs as she yawned, pushing her out the back door.

"Good kitty," she said.

He agreed with one of his hoarse-voiced meows and disappeared inside the store. Feeling completely out of it, she stumbled over to her counter and pulled the Peter the Great book out from under the counter. She still had to deliver Snuock's last book.

She decided to drive. She was exhausted, grumpy, over-caffeinated, and wanted to be able to breathe, free of the smoke from the fireworks. She rolled up the windows, turned on the a/c, and drove through entire neighborhoods filled with the smoke. Streaks of light shot overhead and exploded as if right next to the car. Even with the windows rolled up, her throat quickly felt sore and rough.

But finally she was out of town. Down went the windows. She gulped in lungfuls of fresh air, reveling in the relative rarity of crackles, whizzes, and explosions.

When she finally turned onto the mansion's driveway, the night was almost peaceful.

On the way out to the mansion, she had considered for a few moments turning around and going home. Surely Snuock had better things to do tonight than wait up to receive a book. She'd called him before she left. He hadn't answered the phone; nor had he called or texted her back to tell her not to come.

She was just tired enough to look forward to arguing with the man over the rent increases again. As she drove, she tried to rehearse her arguments in her head. The increases were too sudden; he was going to get himself a lot of bad press locally; she still had enough friends back in Manhattan who might be able to put pressure on Snuock's other businesses...no, scratch that last one. She didn't want to stoop to his level. A delay in the increases so that she and the Jerritts could come up with a brilliant plan to grow their sales...what that brilliant plan might be, she didn't know yet, but she was sure that it would be brilliant...

By the time she reached the mansion, she was almost sane again. Getting away from the constant explosions and back into the fresh air had done her a world of good. She'd only passed a few cars along the route; everyone else was at a barbecue or an amateur fireworks show by now...

The gate was open. She drove around the house to the back door, where deliveries were made. She had a feeling that the front door would be locked and that Snuock wouldn't answer the bell; if not, she'd just drop the book off inside the back door with a note, which she scribbled quickly onto a piece of notebook paper and tucked between the pages.

Then she climbed out of the car and walked to the back door.

She pushed the bell and heard it ring. After half a minute, she pressed it again. Nothing.

Somewhere out in the dark, she heard the creak of a screen door. The hairs raised on Angie's neck. She pressed the doorbell again. Still no answer.

"Hello? Is someone there?" A voice carried through the darkness. Angie turned around to see a flashlight bobbing toward her. She shaded her eyes with her hand, clenched the book with her other hand, and waited.

Valerie walked across the path from the caretaker's lodge. Angie felt herself relax a bit. When Valerie reached the circle of light around the main house's back door, she switched off the flashlight.

"Is something the matter, Ms. Prouty?"

Again with the formal tone.

"I forgot one of the books," Angie said.

"And you thought you'd drop it off now?" Valerie asked incredulously.

Angie didn't know what to say. She checked her phone—it was just past eleven. "Oh. Stupid of me."

"How did you even get up here?"

"I drove in."

"Past the closed gate?"

"Of course not. It was open."

Valerie's eyes widened. "Open?" She looked around, as if searching for another car. "He didn't say he was having visitors. Maybe…"

The two of them turned toward the back door. Valerie reached for the handle—Angie stopped her. Her gut had gone cold as ice.

"Don't touch it," she said. "There might be fingerprints."

"Fingerprints," Valerie said. "What do you think this is, a crime scene?"

Well of course, thought Angie, how could Valerie *not* expect a crime? Angie pulled her sleeve down over her hand, clumsily trying to open the door without disturbing any prints, and failing miserably. Her thumb slipped and rubbed right over the latch.

The door opened; it hadn't been locked.

"I locked that yesterday," Valerie said. "I *locked* that. Myself. With my key. I pulled it closed with my own hand and closed it. With my own key."

You see, Angie wanted to say. Instead she just pushed the door open. It creaked as it swung on its hinges.

"Gotta oil that," Valerie said.

"It's probably just all the smoke in the air."

They walked inside. A few lights were on, none in the hallway, but one in the kitchen.

"Don't touch the switch," Angie said.

"If you really think something bad has happened, we shouldn't be in here. We should be calling the cops."

But Valerie didn't pull out her phone. Neither did Angie. The power of curiosity was just too strong.

The two of them slowly walked through the rooms, using their phones as flashlights when needed, touching nothing. Nothing seemed unordinary or out of place.

"Upstairs?"

They went up, both of them barely making a noise over a whisper. When Valerie called, "Mr. Snuock? Are you all right?" at the top of the stairs, Angie nearly had a heart attack.

The two of them looked from room to room.

The lights were off in the bedroom, and the bed hadn't been made. The bathroom door was open.

Angie made a face. If he'd had a sudden heart attack, the bathroom would be the most likely place. She didn't relish the idea of finding him there.

But if he'd had a heart attack, why would the gate be open?

They stopped at the room at the end of the hall. The study.

The door was shut and a light shone underneath it.

"Mr. Snuock?" Valerie called. "Are you all right?"

No answer.

Valerie reached toward the handle, but stopped herself. She glanced into one of the side rooms, spotted a scarf on a side table, and picked it up to use it to open the door.

Which creaked as it opened.

Great, every door has to creak tonight, Angie thought.

Valerie gasped and froze.

With her hand still wrapped up in her sleeve, Angie reached forward and pushed at the door, opening it the rest of the way.

At the far end of the room, Alexander Snuock lay on the floor. Blood soaked into the carpet. His new Russian presentation pistol lay next to him. It was unbelievable. A *crime* scene, thought Angie. A mix of horror and excitement shot through her.

The blood wasn't bright red and fresh, but other than that...Angie had no way of knowing how long he had been there.

She could see his waxen, pale face. He looked surprised, even...embarrassed.

Angie and Valerie both pulled out their phones at the same time. Angie quickly switched her phone from flashlight to photo mode and snapped some pictures. It was imperative, she reasoned, to get crime scene photos before any evidence be sullied by the elements or negligent detectives.

Valerie, who was clearly the better human being, called 911.

"Hello?" Her voice was shaky. "Hello? I need to report a murder. It's on Polpis Road...it's Mr. Snuock. He's dead."

Chapter 5

CUI BONO? WHO BENEFITS?

It had been a long night with absolutely zero sleep, and Angie had to face at least half a day's worth of work at the bookstore. *Had* to, because today was likely to be a day filled with huge sales, at least for her. After all the work she'd done during the festival to raise awareness of her bookstore, she couldn't just close the shop.

The rent increases might not go through...but then again, they might.

The police had questioned her and Valerie for hours, and then Angie had dragged herself back to the bookstore to unpack the rental trailer so she could deliver it back that morning.

Jo had reacted with shock when she had seen the look on Angie's face. "What happened?"

Angie told her. Jo whistled. "Wow...So we're in the clear for rent?"

It was a heartless thing to say, but Angie understood. Snuock had been threatening Jo's livelihood, her lifelong dream. It had to be on the top of her mind.

"Maybe, maybe not. It depends on whether he set up the next billing cycle already or not."

"But we didn't sign anything agreeing to a new rental rate. Doesn't he have to get a signature or something?"

"I would think so, but...you know what he was like. He might have found some kind of loophole."

"True." Jo chewed on a thumbnail. "It would be just like him, to find a way to screw us over, even after death. When is Aunt Margery coming in to take over for you? You look dead on your feet."

Angie paused in the middle of her third shot of espresso. "I don't know."

"Have you called her yet?"

"I haven't even been *home* yet."

"I'll call her." Jo whipped out her phone and dialed.

"Don't wake her up!"

"She can wake up for this," Jo said grimly. "Hello? Aunt Margery? Have you heard about Alexander Snuock?" She paused. "Yeah, well, it was Angie who found him, and she hasn't had a wink of sleep all night, and now she's arguing with me about calling you to come in early, because she's an idiot. Yeah, I'll stay put for as long as I can and make sure she doesn't do anything stupid. You can get the details when you get here."

She hung up.

Someone knocked at the front door. Jo shouted, "We're not open yet!" and turned back to Angie. Angie stuck her head out of the back room and spotted someone at the door, holding up a police badge.

"I'll be right there!"

She trotted over and unlocked the door. “Yes? Is something wrong? Did I forget something at the festival yesterday? I’ll move the trailer in a few minutes, I promise.”

Her mind had gone completely blank.

“I know you’ve already answered a lot of questions, ma’am, but I have some more for you. About Mr. Snuock’s death.”

She blinked and swayed on her feet. For a moment, she had completely forgotten. She was going to fall asleep standing on her feet.

“Of course. Come in—would you like some coffee?”

“Thank you.”

Jo had melted out of sight and was probably recording the officer on her phone.

Angie tried not to think about that. The officer, who was dressed in a suit rather than a uniform, had dark hair and a five o’clock shadow—cute, if a little a scruffy around the edges. She poured him a cup of coffee and tracked down the last of the cream. She’d have to send Aunt Margery out for more when she arrived. She hoped the officer didn’t keep her tied up until she had to open.

“Can you tell me where you were last night at nine-thirty?” he asked.

“I was still here at the festival, packing up. I didn’t leave here until about ten-twenty.”

“And then you drove to the Snuock home?”

“Yes…”

He ran through a lot of questions that she’d already been asked at the station the previous night. Then he doubled back and started asking her questions about earlier in the day. She was *definitely* not going to finish up before the shop opened for the morning.

She gave the officer—she *knew* she should know his name, but couldn't put her finger on it—the details of the previous day: when she'd arrived, set up, gone to lunch, returned, sent Aunt Margery home, met with Walter Snuock and—

"You met with Walter Snuock?"

Because the officer asked her to, she backed up and told him about their meeting at the bookstore the previous day, and also their errand-running date over lunch. "We were in middle school together," she said lamely. "And it was taking a while to catch up on old times."

The officer wrote a few notes down, then said, "Go on."

She finished her story—Walter missing from the booth when she returned with the trailer, the note he'd left behind—

"Do you still have the note?" the officer asked.

Goosebumps rose along her arms. "Is he all right?" But of course she knew the officer didn't care if Walter was all right, he was just making a list of suspects. A feeling of dread spread through her: Walter wasn't a murderer...was he? She shook the thought out of her head.

"The note?"

"It's probably in my cash bag." She vaguely remembered shoving it inside. She retrieved the bag, opened it, and held it out to the officer without touching the rumpled note shoved inside.

The officer pulled out a pair of latex gloves and a plastic freezer bag. Her heart sank. He gingerly pulled the note out of her cash bag and spread it out in front of him, skimming the note. "I'll have to take this," he said, and placed the note inside the bag, jotting a code on it in permanent marker—then gave her a receipt.

"Please, officer. Tell me what happened. Is Walter all right? Has he been hurt, too?"

He gave her a calm, assessing look. "It's Detective Bailey, ma'am. Please finish your story first."

From a corner of the room, Captain Parfait gave a questioning meow and walked toward her until he was standing at her ankle, butting her in the leg. She picked him up; he glared at Detective Bailey but didn't hiss.

Detective Bailey took a sip of his coffee and stared back.

She went back over her story again. Detective Bailey was going to keep her there all day.

"I...I loaded up the trailer, took down the tent, and dumped the coffee down the storm water drain," she said. "There were fireworks going off, but not the official town ones. The sun had set but it wasn't full dark yet. Almost all the other booths had been packed up by then. It took me longer because of the books."

"I see," he said. "And then?"

"And then I drove back to the bookstore, left the trailer in the back lot—"

"Do you know if there's a camera that covers the back lot, ma'am?"

"You'd have to ask the property manager, Bob Fenton. I have his number somewhere around here—"

She had almost said, *in the back room*, but then suddenly remembered that Jo was probably still there, spying on them. She started to look on the shelves on the wall under the telephone.

"Never mind that," Detective Bailey said. "What time did you leave for Mr. Snuock's house?"

"Ten twenty, I told you."

He made her go over the details again: When had she called Snuock to tell him she was coming to drop off the book? When had she driven past the front gate? When had Valerie come to meet her at the back door? On and on...

By the time she had finished catching up to this morning, she was hoarse.

Detective Bailey said, "Did you see your great-aunt this morning?"

"No, I never made it home. She should be in soon."

"Did you see any of the other tenants this morning?"

"Tenants?"

"The other people who are renting from Mr. Snuock."

"I saw Josephine Jerritt this morning when she dropped off the pastries as usual. She was going to stick around for a while...but I think she's gone."

"When did she leave?"

"I don't know. After you got here? At the same time? I think she didn't want to intrude. Why? Is she a suspect? Am I a suspect?" Angie's head was spinning.

"Let's just say you're a person of interest."

"Do you know who did it? Do you have any actual suspects?"

The detective shook his head. "I can't talk about that, ma'am."

Of course he couldn't. She was sick to her stomach. "You think Walter did it."

"We're just collecting information, ma'am."

Angie could tell that he wanted to tell her to calm down and get a grip. Fortunately he didn't; she might have lost it at that point. She took a deep breath.

"What do you need me to do?"

"Please don't leave the island for the next few days without telling us. We need to be able to reach you at all times—keep your cell phone at hand."

"He was shot because it was the fourth," she said suddenly then regretted it. But she was so tired. It was impossible to keep from blurting things out loud.

Detective Bailey was suddenly more attentive than he had been the entire interview: "What makes you say that?"

"The Fourth of July, with all of those fireworks going off. A mystery reader like me, you have to think—it would be the perfect occasion to shoot someone. Nobody would know that it wasn't just fireworks, especially with the house all the way up on the hill like that. Nobody would have a clue."

#

After Angie wrapped up with Detective Bailey, she checked the back room. Jo was gone. Neither the front nor back doors had bells on them; Angie hated to interrupt her customers just as they were getting sucked into a book, and had taken them off when she'd leased the store.

She was completely out of time to return the trailer or to pick up cream. She managed to get the rolling bookshelves unloaded from the trailer and in the back door, but more than that would have to wait until Aunt Margery arrived.

Which was in short order. Aunt Margery appeared at the back door, looking flustered and tired, but cheerfully willing to help finish opening the shop so Angie could get home and rest. She managed not to waste time picking Angie's brain for details, other than that Angie and Valerie had seen the body. Angie gave her the phone and let her look at the photos she'd taken. She'd been so upset that half the photos were blocked by Valerie's shoulder. Oh well. At least she'd taken a few good ones.

She probably should have mentioned them to the officers the previous night or Detective Bailey this morning. Maybe after she slept...

Unfortunately, she didn't have a number for Walter, so she couldn't check on him. So she brewed coffee, shoved the rolling shelves into the back, and opened up for the day, reminding herself that this was *not* a smart day to leave the shop closed. In fact, she wasn't sure when she'd have a day off. She intended to keep the shop open extended hours until the foot traffic died down a bit, then she'd start giving Aunt Margery days off, and then...well, she might not have a day off until September.

The morning rush was actually a rush: there was a line for coffee and pastries. She set out a dish with a pile of quarters and a note saying that plain coffee was fifty cents, with another fifty cents for soy milk (sorry no cream today) and please leave a tip—she was too swamped with espresso orders to do anything else, and the last thing she wanted was to turn anyone away *today*, after all her hard work and money spent on fliers and custom coffee cups. She sold a few newspapers with the coffee. One of the patrons asked if she had any local advertising papers with garage sales. Another asked for a particular magazine. Soon the shop was buzzing with people sitting at tables—tourists doubled up with locals and chatting. Aunt Margery ran the register while Angie pulled shots and built drinks.

She was hot and tired before it was seven, and smiling, despite her desire to lie down and sleep on the floor behind the counter.

Some days were bad days, when she castigated herself for quitting the investment firm in Manhattan and leaving her obviously marked-for-success boyfriend—it would have been a compromised life, but an easier one...in some ways. Then there were days like this when she felt like she was bringing some good to the world *and* making a profit.

Mickey strode past the window—his tall head bobbing over the top of the shelves—and glanced in at the pastry case, then disappeared. A few minutes later, Jo came in the back door with a tray of fresh donuts. "Fifty cents each," she called. "Pay at the register when you get a moment. Nantucket Bakery down the street, a partner of Pastries & Page-Turners!"

Laughter and cheering went up—and the donuts disappeared.

Jo returned with additional trays of pastries while the people in the café area were still licking their fingers. A young boy, staring at Jo's hair, told his mother, "That lady's hair looks like green frosting."

"There's a thought," Angie muttered to her friend. "You should sell green frosted donuts and call them à la Josephine."

"Makes me sound French," she said. "So...about the visitor you had earlier this morning?""

Angie didn't want to say anything out loud in front of the customers, so she nodded.

"You're all covered?"

That must be Jo code for, "And you have an alibi for the time in question?" It wasn't an idle question, either. Jo had lied for Angie a couple of times while they were in high school—without Angie finding out about it until later.

"No," Angie said. "Not covered at all."

"What?"

A couple of customers looked up. Angie rang up a woman at the counter who wanted two Danishes and a caramel mocha latte. A lot of sugar, so early in the morning, but she was on vacation. Why not?

"I was there, Jo," Angie told her over the screech of the steamer wand in the milk pitcher. "I have to be, um, not covered. But it seemed like what he was *really* interested in were the other people I spent time with yesterday."

She finished the shot just as Jo shouted, "Who was that?"

Now everyone was looking their way, including Aunt Margery. She had been almost suspiciously quiet and incurious this morning, as a matter of fact. Angie snorted and assembled the drink, stirring it carefully, then topping it with whipped cream, chocolate shavings, and a swirl of caramel—a drink she had done so often she could do it in her sleep, which she very nearly was.

The woman sipped at her caramel mocha and smiled. Loudly, she said, "Thank you! Now I'm ready to drive back to Maryland."

Angie whistled and said, "Long drive. Are you sure you don't want an extra shot?"

The people in the café laughed and finally went back to minding their own business.

"Walter," Angie told Jo.

"Walter Snuock?" Jo hissed. "You were with *him* yesterday? After everything his father is doing right now?"

"He doesn't like his father any better than you do," Angie said.

"Oh, he might *say* that. But where do you think his inheritance is coming from?"

They both paused: Angie because the comment was in bad taste; Jo probably because she was wondering if a murder investigation would hold up an inheritance. She had that kind of mind, anyway.

"It must have happened during the fireworks show," Jo said.

Exactly what Angie had been thinking.

Another customer came up to the counter and ordered a dry cappuccino, to go. "How far to go?" she asked.

"Just up and down the street," he said.

She made a face, considering. He was about sixty years old and had a *Wall Street Journal* under one arm. "All the tables are full, aren't they?" she asked. "I can trust you to bring the cup back, right?"

He smiled and she made the cappuccino in a proper cup, quickly making a feather pattern in the foam as she poured it. He smiled again, and a five-dollar tip might have made its way into the tip jar.

"What do you think about breakfast sandwiches?" she asked Jo.

"Are you changing the subject?"

"A little."

"Why didn't you just give the guy a cappuccino in a to-go cup like he asked?"

"Because people who ask for dry cappuccinos don't want to-go cups. Not really."

Jo rolled her eyes. "I just know pastries and gossip."

"You have to get used to glancing people over and getting a feel for them very quickly."

"I suppose you know who the shoplifters are going to be, too."

"Sometimes," Angie said smugly.

"I think breakfast sandwiches would be a good idea for the bakery," Jo hedged.

"But not for the bookshop?"

"You don't have an oven. And wouldn't you need to get different permits for that?"

Angie opened her mouth then snapped it shut. She had almost said, *now that we're not getting a rent increase, I might have some extra cash lying around*. Which was ghoulish. But there it was: one of the reasons that she logically had to be a suspect, even if she hadn't been one of the two people to find a body.

Which meant...the other shop owners had to be suspects, too.

Like Jo.

Would she have killed someone in order to protect the bakery and her brother?

Angie wanted to say no. The murder had been well planned: otherwise, why use the fireworks for cover? Although, *that* was exactly the kind of thinking Jo might put into a job like this. Mickey? Angie wouldn't have suspected him in a million years.

Angie felt chilled; she couldn't believe she was considering her best friend in this way. But to get to the bottom of any case one had to remain dispassionate and consider all suspects.

Suspecting Jo hadn't taken more than a few minutes.

#

Finally the coffee sales tapered off. The café wasn't packed solid, but all the comfy chairs in the store were filled with customers contentedly reading books. Captain Parfait had poked his head out to check on a crying baby, but had otherwise stayed out of sight.

Aunt Margery gave Angie a peck on her cheek. "I think I can manage from here. Go ahead and pick up the cream...then go home and take a nap."

"I have to drop off the trailer as well. Will you be all right?"

Aunt Margery's eyebrows went up: "Of course. You should be asking yourself that question…I'm sorry you had to find Snuock like you did."

"It's not your fault."

A shadow seemed to pass over Aunt Margery's face. "No, it's not." Then it was gone, replaced by her usual resoluteness. "Now you go and take care of yourself. Get going."

Angie hesitated. "Aunt Margery, I have to know…have your friends told you what happened to Walter? Is he all right?"

"Oh, he's fine. He's at his mother's house. He's been told not to leave town."

"They don't think he did it," Angie said. "That's good."

"I didn't say *that*," Aunt Margery said. "Detective Bailey has always been one to keep secrets close to his chest."

Angie frowned at her.

"Didn't you know? He's a local. Of course, he's five years older than you. Lived here most of his life, but he was out at college while you were in high school…yes, that's it. Children are so insular. If they weren't in the same class, it was as if other people didn't exist."

Angie couldn't argue with that. "Bailey's not a usual name around here, is it?"

"It used to be. His parents came here to find their roots after a few generations away. It's the housing prices, I suppose. They drive a number of people away."

Angie shook her head. Her great-aunt was distracting her with interesting information—she had to get back on track. "But Walter?"

"Oh, yes, well. *He* has a motive."

"Just because you don't like your father doesn't mean that you want to murder him."

"It might, if he were cutting off your allowance."

Angie frowned. She vaguely remembered something about that. "What was that all about, anyway?"

"Alexander accused Phyllis of conceiving Walter with another man. Then refused to accept the results of the DNA test she had done for him."

"What?"

"The real issue appeared to be that he thought she was cheating on him."

"Cheating on him? Back then?"

"Back then, and now."

Angie's face was pinched in confusion. "But they've been divorced for years."

"Oh, I know Agnes, it's all some kind of crazy, but that's Alexander Snuock for you."

Several of the customers were very fixedly looking at their books without turning the pages: most of them were tourists, so Angie supposed the story wouldn't travel very far, but still. She said, "We should talk about this later."

"We should."

Angie's mind was reeling as she left the shop. So Mr. Alexander Snuock was such a control freak that he kept tabs on his ex-wife's love life, and insisted that she not have any lovers or else...he'd go as far as disinheriting their son, asserting Walter might not even be his. Hadn't he even considered how much something like that would hurt *Walter*? Why not just cut off Phyllis's alimony—she must have reaped quite a package from Snuock; although, as Angie thought about it, the alimony was probably wrapped-up tightly in legalities, impossible to touch. Still, what a madman.

#

While Angie was out running errands, her phone rang with an unrecognized number from out of her area code. She almost let it go to voice mail, then suddenly pulled over to the shoulder and changed her mind.

"Hello? Angie Prouty speaking."

"Angie? This is Walter."

She was so startled that the car jerked forward. She put the car into park, set the brake, and turned off the engine.

"Walter! Are you all right?"

"I'm fine. I wanted to check on you," he said.

"I'm fine," said Angie. "The police have told me to not leave town any time soon, but that's about it. I'm fine. How are you?"

Walter drew a ragged breath. "Okay, I just *said* I was fine, but—"

"But you're not," she said. "You need food and a sympathetic ear, and I'm not a terrible cook. Let me call Aunt Margery and make sure she's all right, and then you can come over to my place for lunch and sanity."

"I don't know if I need lunch," he said, "but some sanity would be nice."

In twenty minutes he was wolfing down a French omelet with crusty bread and a simple, mustardy salad with farmers' market tomatoes. She made him a second omelet, and that one disappeared in short order, too.

"I didn't realize I was so hungry," he said.

"That's grief for you," she said. She'd been here when Mickey and Jo's father, Hank, had passed—almost exactly a year ago. She was no pastry chef, so she couldn't have run the bakery for the twins even if she had wanted to. Somehow, Dory had stepped into place for them, mindlessly and robotically making breads and pastries as her children made the funeral arrangements. Angie had kept them all fed, spending more time organizing all the sympathy casseroles than actually cooking herself. All three of them had eaten like wolves for weeks straight. Some people didn't eat when they grieved, but not the Jerritts: they burned at both ends and ate like it, too.

"They're doing an autopsy," Walter said.

"Walter, they're not telling me anything that I didn't see with my own two eyes. Was it a burglar?"

He shook his head. "Whoever did it didn't force his way in." In a choked voice, he added, "They walked me through the house to see whether anything was out of place. I saw them. The same books that you picked out for me."

It hit her how it might have seemed to him. She said, "Sorry. I do that—once I bother to spend time researching a particular area of books, then I recommend the living daylights out of them. To everyone. Because at least I know they're good books. You just happened to be looking for the same ones."

Walter sighed and took a drink of water, starting with a sip—then gulped the rest of the glass down. She poured him another one and he drank that, too. He seemed bereft. She wouldn't let herself think of him as a suspect. Sure, she could argue he had a motive, but his motive fit too perfectly—an angry and rejected son who stood to lose his inheritance—and he was too smart; he knew he'd be the first person people would suspect. So it just couldn't be him.

"Do you need to lie down? Have you slept?" she asked. She personally had gone so far past her bedtime that it seemed like she would never sleep again.

"I haven't," he admitted. "But I've got a room at Jellicoe House now."

Jellicoe House was a B&B south of town, off Old South Road, the kind of place with patterned silk wallpaper and a thousand antiques, with a big wraparound porch, close enough to bike to the south beaches, and close to the airport.

"Can I drive you?"

"I'm fine," he said. "Fine to drive, anyway."

She offered him the tiny guest bed anyway, but he refused and took off in his rental car. She watched him until he was gone, and then went upstairs to take a quick shower and change clothes. She'd be fine to keep going until the bookstore closed for the day...at least she should go back and deliver the cream.

One blink and she found herself underneath her quilt with all her clothes on, including her shoes. Her eyes were already half closed.

She took off her shoes without sitting up, sliding them off her feet and kicking them out from under the covers. She was too tired to care.

Too tired to do anything but sleep.

#

It was six o'clock in the evening. Angie still felt woozy from waking up at a strange time of day, but at least she'd made it back to the bookstore and delivered the cream—better late than never.

"Well?" Aunt Margery asked.

"Well what?"

"What's his alibi?"

Angie shook her head. "I wasn't under the impression that I was supposed to be questioning the man."

"Don't play the fool with me, girl. You weren't raised on fairy tales."

Actually, she had been, but now was not the time to point that out. "He's staying at the Jellicoe."

Aunt Margery grunted. "At least you found that out. Did you feed him?"

"Two omelets."

"Good girl. He probably doesn't know up from down at this point. But he was always a good kid. You can tell by his behavior that his parents getting divorced didn't spoil him out of it. I hope he doesn't get in trouble."

Angie's shoulders relaxed. "So you don't think he did it?" They were in the back room, speaking in low voices—it was more private; however, in a moment, Angie would have to check on her customers in the front.

"No," Aunt Margery said. "Mind you, I couldn't produce any evidence to prove it, but I'd wager he didn't have anything to do with it. I know the Snuocks. Either they're the Machiavellian type or the feudal lord type—the good kind, if there is such a thing. Very well-intentioned, at any rate. I'd put Walter in the well-intentioned feudal lord camp with no real appetite for murder.

"Seriously?" Angie asked. "How do you know all of this?"

Aunt Margery let out an exasperated sigh. "I've been on this island forever.

"And what if he takes after his mother?" Angie asked

Aunt Margery glared at her. "Do I look like I keep a Nantucket breeding book handy? Like a dog-breeder keeping an eye on his dogs' tempers?" She grimaced. "Don't answer that."

#

The Nantucket Bakery was closed for the day, but of course the twins were still inside, working.

Mickey sat on a stool in the back, decorating a cake.

"Someone's wedding?" Angie asked.

The cake was three tiers, covered with purple frosting and—she squinted—black spiders.

"No," he said, a little deflated. "I just got bored. How many Goths do we have in Nantucket?"

"So you're decorating a cake for fun?"

"Not just any cake, a display cake. It's just Styrofoam in there. And, you know. Sugar. It'll last until Halloween and get people thinking, hey, you know what sounds good for Halloween? A really expensive, elaborately decorated cake."

It was one of those moments where she couldn't decide whether Mickey was being serious or ironic. He lay the airbrush down and put his chin in his hand, tilting his head to look at the cake.

He shifted on the stool and glanced at her. "I heard the cops came to talk to you, too," Mickey said. "They would have to though, you did find the body. Do you know if you're a suspect?"

"They haven't taken me down to the station and fingerprinted me," she said.

"You could have shot him, left, and come back again."

"Really, Mickey?" She didn't hide the irritation in her voice.

"Sorry," he said, a little remorsefully, and pressed a large plastic spider into the side of the cake. "I hated the guy, but wouldn't wish him dead. The whole thing is kind of mind blowing."

"Yes, it is. And we're all suspects. So you better have your story straight." She still felt wonky, what a tactless things to say.

He gave her a level look. "I was here by myself. At least Jo was staying over at Mom's."

Of course Mickey would never think of making up a story or twisting the truth to establish an alibi. His good nature overrode his instinct for self-preservation. It's what she loved about him and what also drove her crazy.

He framed his hands in front of the cake like a viewfinder. "So I'm thinking the very top of this will be a haunted house, and the next layer will be a graveyard."

"What about the bottom layer?"

"I thought about doing flames, but, you know, I think that's kind of expected, and honestly, they're not that challenging to do."

"A wrought-iron fence with a cool gate?"

"That might work." He paused, studying the cake. "Jo was saying that Walter doesn't have an alibi for Friday night—he was out all over the island trying to track down his mother."

Casually, she asked, "Oh?" And wondered if Mickey knew that she'd been out on what could be construed as a date with Walter recently.

In the same tone, he said, "Yeah. Apparently she called him and said it was an emergency. I heard that he drove over to Snuock Manor thinking she might be there. The gate was open, so he drove up to the house. When he didn't see his mom's car there, he turned around and went back, then spent the rest of the night looking for her."

That would have been before she and Valerie had found the body. If he had driven to Snuock Manor Angie likely would have seen him on the road returning to town as she drove out there that very night, not too long after he'd heard from his mother. Jo had either completely embellished the few details Angie gave her or she had another source. And it's not as if Phyllis or Walter would sit down and have a powwow with Jo, or anyone else for that matter, and give away details that would implicate them. It all sounded like conjecture to her.

"Who were Jo's sources?"

"She never tells me," Mickey said.

"That's because you don't care," Jo said, coming into the kitchen from the back, drying her hands on a towel. Her green hair seemed to glow through her hairnet. "Heya, Angie."

"Heya, Jo. What's the story?"

"I talked to Mom, actually. She says that the only thing keeping Walter out of jail is the fact that there's no physical evidence tying him to the actual scene of the crime."

"Wow," said Angie. She wasn't surprised about the lack of physical evidence, but she was surprised Dory Jerritt knew as much as she did. It begged the question, how?

"So watch your back if you decide to go out with him again."

Mickey straightened up. "You're going out with *him*? After what his father did to our rent?"

Angie gritted her teeth and gave Jo an accusatory look. Didn't she know old flames die hard and that Angie and Mickey's friendship rested on treading lightly around each other; the fewer details they shared about who they were seeing, the better.

Jo slapped Mickey on the shoulder. “Be nice to the woman. Who do you think is going to convince his son to change his mind about the rent?”

Angie wanted to throw up her hands. Jo really knew how to dig a hole.

Mickey swallowed his disapproval and turned to Angie. “Want some cake?”

Chapter 6

PLAYING TWENTY QUESTIONS

If a criminal has to have a motive in order to commit a crime, then an amateur detective had to have a motive to try to solve it.

Was it a Prouty thing, being nosy? Did an instinct for this kind of thing run in the family, along with sea captains and wanderlust?

Was she trying to defend herself from accusations of murder (that nobody would seriously consider; after all, if she had intended to kill Snuock in a rage she had had a perfect opportunity the day before his actual murder)?

Was she trying to defend Jo from accusations of murder (when she already had an alibi)?

Or was she trying to prove Walter's innocence, to herself, if not to the police?

She made a face. She *did* like him. And she could rarely help trying to provide comfort and assistance to people she liked. Besides, he couldn't be a murderer because what would that say about her judgment and instincts?

Maybe she should leave it to the police. After all, what was she going to be able to do? She didn't have a forensics team behind her; had no training whatsoever in handling evidence, let alone finding it; didn't have a clue when it came to legal procedures; and was only able to solve about a third of the Agatha Christie novels on her first pass (and forgot an embarrassing number of plotlines and titles, which led to her throwing down a book more than once with the conviction, "Aha! I know who the killer is now," only to realize a chapter later that she'd read the book before).

Nosiness wasn't about being competent (though she did consider herself competent). It was just about an insatiable need to know—another trait that ran in the Prouty family.

After leaving the bakery, Angie found herself wandering along the backs of the buildings through the alleyway. A few of the local artists had painted on the bricks of the buildings inside bricked-up windows. The old window arches provided an impromptu kind of frame. The reason for it was practical as much as it was artistic—graffiti artists tended not to disturb buildings that had art on them. A few walls did have tags, layers upon layers of them, as the taggers—who were mostly local high school students anyway—competed to stay on top as long as possible.

A car made its way slowly down the alley, and Angie backed up against a store's back doorway to get out of the way. Inside the car was Dory Jerritt, looking cross and worried. A lot on her mind, thought Angie. It couldn't hurt to see where Dory was going, surely, and see if she had a moment to talk.

#

Angie caught up with Dory at the door of Pastries & Page-Turners, of all places. She wasn't bringing pastries with her in the car, so Angie decided she must be fair game. Why drive from the bakery to the bookstore, though. And why use the back alley?

She must want to have a private word with Aunt Margery after closing, which would be at eight that evening. Maybe the two of them would go out to supper…

“Hello, Dory,” Angie said, coming up behind her at the back door of the bookstore.

Dory jumped.

“Hello, kiddo,” she said. “I didn’t see you back there. You nearly scared the crap out of me.”

“I’m sorry! I certainly didn’t mean to. Looking for Aunt Margery?”

“We’re going out this evening after work. I thought I’d stop by and help her close up, hurry things along a bit. That woman really knows how to drag her feet.”

Dory Jerritt wasn’t the most tactful person in the world, but then again she wasn’t wrong.

“I’m sure she’ll be glad for the help,” Angie said. “I was planning to do the same thing.”

“How are you feeling?” Dory’s eyes narrowed with a genuine look of concern.

It was always best to assume that Dory, like Aunt Margery’s other friends, knew everything that Aunt Margery knew: “Better. I slept like a log. I barely even remembered to take my shoes off.”

Dory gave her a tsk tsk. “You need to take better care of yourself.”

“I suppose so. How did things go the other night with Jo?”

Dory took a deep breath. The two of them were still standing outside the back door of the shop; unless Aunt Margery spotted them and came out to interrupt, Dory couldn’t escape without being rude.

“The other night with Jo?”

"I know the two of you have had...a few arguments about things."

This was a pretty safe statement; the two of them didn't get along as well as they could. Both women were confrontational and direct, yet had completely different philosophies about how one's life should be led, from the color of one's hair to the way one made crepes. Sometimes Angie wanted to shake them and tell them that they were more similar than they realized, but that would have just made both of them turn on her to support each other's arguments about how different they were. There was no logic. Family, Angie thought.

"Oh," Dory said. "Yes, I went over to her apartment on Thursday night and we made spaghetti. She asked Mickey if he wanted to come over and make a family night of it. He said he was too busy designing Halloween decorations and didn't want to intrude on girl talk."

Angie chuckled, that sounded just like him. And Dory's explanation checked out—Jo had just said that she was at her mother's house that evening—but she'd paused before giving it. Wait. Did Dory go over to Jo's or did Jo go over to Dory's? A minor detail, but telling nonetheless, Angie thought.

What were the two of them covering up?

And if she pressed Mickey, what story would come out? Probably the same one as Dory's now, because she would have asked him to cover up for her and Jo. He was prone to tell the truth without thinking, but he'd lie to protect Jo.

"That sounds fun," Angie said. "Too bad that I was out on a date."

"I heard about that. Walter Snuock," Dory said, with obvious pleasure of being up-to-date on the gossip already. "What did you think of him?"

Angie's face turned warm. She hoped she wasn't blushing. "I thought he was interesting and polite."

"Uh-huh. And not likely to take credit for your work," Dory said.

"Ach," Angie said, putting her hands over her heart and pretending to take a mortal wound. "Thanks so much for reminding me."

Dory laughed. "Don't worry. You still have time to fall in love. It's not like there's only one fish in the sea."

"I'd be happy to find my first real fish," Angie said. "That first one, he was a shark. I don't think he counts."

"I'm glad to hear that you haven't let a bad romantic experience weigh you down…when you first moved here, we were all worried about you."

"Were you?"

"Of course. You'd always been such a solitary, serious child. Nose in a book, studying or reading. But you have always been a good friend to my children, so I knew that you had a good heart in you."

"Thank you," Angie said, genuinely touched.

"And now that you're dating again…well, even if things don't work out with Walter, at least you know that you're over what's-his-name for good."

Angie restrained a smile. "Walter was only here to try to patch things up between his mother and father, from what he says, and now…My guess is that he'll stay here long enough for the funeral, and then make a break for it. I think I would."

For a moment, Dory looked stricken. "Oh, I'm so sorry! I didn't mean to bring up a painful subject."

"It's all right." Dory's lack of tact was simply part and parcel of talking to her best friends' mother, and she'd become used to it years and years ago. "It's just one of those things that's not meant to be. Bad timing."

"Well, I hope he at least cancels the rent increase on your property."

"What about everyone else's?"

"That's probably too much to hope for."

Which was true. The back door opened, and Aunt Margery leaned out. "Why, Dory! Are you here to collect me? It's too early. I haven't even closed up shop yet, and I'll be some time putting things in order for Angie in the morning. You know she's had a very difficult day, and I wouldn't want to leave her with a pile of worries first thing in the morning."

"Margery, you've been hoping and praying that I'd show up early to help you get yourself sorted, and don't deny it! Every time we go out for supper, you drag your feet for so long that I'm eventually forced to help out if I want to eat before midnight!"

Aunt Margery winked at Angie. "That simply isn't true, and you know it. I am merely being thoughtful."

Angie said, "You're as thoughtful as the day is long."

"Which day?" Aunt Margery grumbled. "Midwinter over the Arctic Circle?"

Dory said, "Oh, Margery, love, that reminds me, do you know who I saw marching around downtown today?"

"An army?"

"Ray. He's mad enough to spit nails."

"Ray?" For a moment Aunt Margery looked as though she had never heard of the man. Then her eyebrows rose and she gave a low whistle. "And here I would have thought that he would have been pleased, what with Alexander's death and all."

"Yes, you would have thought."

The two of them paused awkwardly, and stared at each other.

“Why do you think he was in such a temper?” Aunt Margery asked.

“No idea,” Dory said.

“If you had to guess...?”

“If I *had* to guess, I’d say that the man couldn’t find the bright side to winning the lottery. He’d complain about taxes for the rest of his life, and how they stole most of ‘his’ money.”

“You know,” Aunt Margery said, “That feud between him and Alexander goes back to that day when...”

“Oh, yes,” Dory said.

Angie’s interest was piqued. She started to feel like she was watching a play, one with a few lines of audience participation. “What feud?” she asked. “It must have been pretty serious for two grown men to hang onto it for so many years.”

Aunt Margery stood in the doorway, put her finger against her nose and said, “‘But it isn’t old!’ Tweedledum cried, in a greater fury than ever. ‘It’s new, I tell you—I bought it yesterday—my nice NEW RATTLE!’”

“Alice in Wonderland!” Dory said.

“You got one! Finally!” Said Aunt Margery with a roll of the eyes.

Dory shook her head. “I don’t know why I bother speaking to you. You can’t stop quoting books I haven’t read, which is rude, and you’re lazy.”

“Lazy?” Aunt Margery demanded.

It was impossible not to be charmed by them. They had a secret language; who knows what they were really talking about. Their quick wits were a smokescreen to conceal the truth, but Angie was determined that they get back to it.

"Ahem," Angie said. "The feud?"

Aunt Margery's eyes seemed to twinkle. "It wasn't over anything serious, my dear. It comes down to the fact that they never liked each other, that was all."

"Come on. There has to be a reason they never liked each other." Angie prickled with impatience.

"Curiosity killed the cat, you know," Dory said.

"But satisfaction brought it back," both Aunt Margery and Angie said at the same time, which made Dory chortle.

"What did it start with?" Dory asked. "There were so many episodes."

"The boat race?"

"It might have been the boat race. But wasn't that in high school? Surely it had started before that."

Aunt Margery arched an eyebrow toward her friend. "Before *that*?"

"Yes, before *that*," Dory said firmly.

They could have been talking about the boat race, whatever that was, but Angie didn't think so.

"Oh, I know," Aunt Margery said. "They both had a crush on our teacher, don't you remember? Miss Prall."

"Miss Prall! She was six feet tall!" Dory chanted, and they both laughed. "Oh, she was pretty, wasn't she? Or is that just my memory?"

Angie scratched her head. This was like trying to follow the mind of the Mad Hatter.

"I'd have to look it up in the old school photos," Aunt Margery said. "And heaven knows where those are. In the attic somewhere."

"You know exactly where those photos are," Dory said. "You never misplace a thing."

That simply wasn't true, but Angie didn't bother to correct her. She was still wondering what it was that these two women were really trying to accomplish. To tell her something, obviously...but in such a roundabout way that it made her suspicious.

"Or in..." Aunt Margery stared upward into the sunset-orange sky. "No, it wouldn't have been in any of the papers. She only taught those two years—kindergarten with us then moved up to first grade. We were all so enchanted to have her both years."

"I thought she was an angel," Dory announced.

"I remember," Aunt Margery said drily. "But you remember that Alex and Ray were at each other's throats over her? Both of them fighting over her attention, and pleased as punch when they found out the best way to get it was to fight each other?"

"Oh I do," Dory said. "But they were like that in kindergarten, too. One of them couldn't have anything that the other didn't have to have better. Toys, crayons, chairs..."

They both shook their heads.

Okay, thought Angie, now they were getting somewhere: a woman, probably not their teacher, was the source of the tension between Ray and Snuock.

"And the worst part was growing up, knowing that eventually Alex would have to win," Dory said.

"Oh, yes. Every time they fought, it was 'when I grow up I'll be rich and you'll be a nobody' at the end. It must have been maddening," Aunt Margery said.

Then they both looked at Angie.

"What are we doing, standing out here and talking when you should be asleep?" Aunt Margery said.

Sleep was the furthest thing from her mind; she'd only awakened a few hours ago.

"Really, I'm fine," said Angie. She hoped a salient detail would slip out the longer they kept up this charade.

"She needs food, not sleep," Dory insisted.

"Sheldon's always has an extra table or two open for the locals," Aunt Margery said.

"But she's just been," Dory said. "Don't you think she'd rather—"

Angie laughed. "Fine, fine, I'm going! I can pick out my own supper, thank you very much."

Aunt Margery looked at her, tilting her head as if weighing her up. "You should call Walter and see how he's doing."

Hmm. She did have his cell phone number now.

"Perhaps I shall," she said.

"Good. Now off you go...it's eight o'clock already, and I have to start closing up the shop if we're going to get anything to eat before midnight..."

"I won't wait up," Angie said, and took a step back.

Aunt Margery let Dory in, then closed the door tightly, not going as far as to lock it, but urging Angie with a pointed finger toward Angie's car in the parking lot before she disappeared into the shop.

Angie laughed, amused and perplexed by her great-aunt and Dory.

She leaned against her car and admired the orange and red of the evening sky. As she was about to call Walter, the next door down the alley opened. Ruth emerged, struggling with a large bag of trash. Angie jogged over to help.

The bag was heavy. Fortunately it was a heavy-duty bag; otherwise, whatever was inside would have torn out of the bag and spilled all over the sidewalk.

"What's in here, a body?" Angie joked.

"I didn't do it, I wasn't there, and I don't know nothing," Ruth said immediately.

Angie cracked up. "What's with you broads tonight?"

"Oh?"

"First Dory, then Aunt Margery, now you. All three of you are fast on the draw."

Ruth perked up. "Is Dory here?"

"Yes, she and Aunt Margery are closing up the shop. I've been kicked out and told to go back to sleep, when I just woke up at five-thirty."

"You *could* call Walter," Ruth said, brushing a lock of hair away from her face. Her bangles jingled on her wrist. "See if he wants to go out for supper and sympathy."

"Are all three of you in cahoots? Can't you talk about anything else?" It was like a memo went out warning everyone that her spinsterhood was imminent, so would they please do their best to get Angie a date with the most eligible bachelor in town; never mind that he was the most likely suspect in a murder case.

"We're old," Ruth said. "All we think about is sleep, food, and getting all single women younger than us set up with nice young men who have a bit of money to spend. You'll only know what it's like when your child is old enough to have grandchildren. There's a voice whispering in the back of your head...diapers...must have diapers..."

"You think about plenty more than that." Angie bit her lower lip. She was curious about Ruth. All the merchants in town who rented from Snuock had a motive. "Are you going to be all right, by the way? If the rent increase still goes through?"

Ruth looked back and forth along the alleyway then waved Angie inside the back door of her shop. Once inside, she whispered, "Don't let it get around, but the increase is almost sure to go through. Alexander filed the paperwork months ago. I'm sure we'll get letters in the mail in a day or two from the lawyers. You know lawyers, once they have signed paperwork in hand, it's almost impossible to derail them. They'll just argue that it's for the good of the estate."

Angie sighed. Her trip to Greece was receding ever further from the realm of possibility.

"But I'll be fine," Ruth added. "God willing, and fingers-crossed that the Internet auction sites don't get shut down anytime soon. Plus I have a bit tucked away for retirement. No, don't worry about Auntie Ruth."

"I'm glad to hear it."

"What are you going to do about the Jerritt twins?"

"Me?"

"The three of you have always been as thick as thieves. Surely you have some scheme up your sleeve to help them out."

"I haven't really had time to think," Angie admitted. She suddenly felt the burden of responsibility.

"Well, get on it. Those are good kids, even if they're a little proud. Not a patch on their mother, of course—"

"Was it you that she had supper with the other night?" Angie asked. "On Thursday?"

"Thursday? No, why?"

Angie pulled at her bottom lip with her fingers. Something wasn't right.

Ruth chuckled. "Oh, is there hanky-panky going on? I'll have to ask."

"Don't tell her I said anything."

Ruth put a hand on her chest. "What, give away a source? *Me*?"

"You're terrible." Ruth would definitely mention it to Dory. Gossips. Her Aunt Margery was no exception, either. They never told a straight story. It peeved Angie to no end that they didn't let her into the circle.

"I am," said Ruth. "Now, if you have a minute, I need some help with a few other bags..."

Angie's groaning question, "Just what's in here anyway?" was answered variously with, "more dead bodies," "paperwork I'm trying to hide from the IRS," "cartloads of cement from the basement for the tunnel I'm trying to dig under the bank," and "oh, I went to an estate sale and picked up a large lot with a few things I wanted...and a lot of trash I didn't need."

The last reason was the one most likely to be true, but not the only possible one. The packed antique store had everything from crystal chandeliers to racks of silver serving spoons, to an entire row of double-hung silver mirrors, each of them reflecting back on itself. A carousel horse stood next to a Sixteenth-century French armoire; boat paddles rested next to a rack full of handmade lace. A stubby, tiny banjo hung among a set of copper pans, and antique pot-metal ashtrays surrounded a wooden rack filled with printer's letters.

She remembered the day she'd first come into the shop with her parents. The three of them had wandered through the narrow aisles, Angie with her hands held carefully behind her back. It had seemed a magical place. When she found out that she would be able to get the shop next to Ruth's, Angie had been overjoyed.

She hauled the last bag toward the back door and paused to get her breath. The one she was dragging now was the heaviest of the bunch. Ruth must have overfilled it because it was the last one.

Panting, Angie looked up. The far wall of the back room was covered in layers and layers of photographs. The ones near the bottom were black and white with ragged-trim edges. Some color photos, very faded. Above them were scads of Polaroid shots, faded even worse than the color photos below them. Above the polaroids were more recent color photos. The very top layer was made of inkjet color printouts.

Ruth was back at her counter, counting her drawer. Angie could hear the jingle of change and the credit card machine running its nightly batch on its tiny internal printer.

Decades of history were right here: a few snapshots of famous visitors; a lot of photographs of Ruth standing proudly in front of some antique that must have meant a lot to her, shaking hands with a customer as she turned it over; vacation photos of Ruth, Dory, and Aunt Margery standing on the beach.

Using the side of her hand, Angie gently touched some of the pictures to lift the edges so she could look underneath them at the black and white ones on the bottom.

Some of the photos were of children. One of them looked like Angie's father as a boy, dark-haired and staring up at the sky. A thumb's silhouette darkened the edge of the photo. Ruth must have been an amateur shutterbug from a very young age. The photo looked almost secretive, as if Ruth had been taking photos of Angie's father on the sly.

She riffled gently through the photographs, making sure not to knock any of them down. Her fingers stopped on a photo of two people standing next to a boat. She couldn't make out the name of the boat, but at least one of the people looked familiar—a teenaged Dory. Her face looked like Josephine's had in high school, minus the strange haircut. She looked almost waifish. The day must have been windy; she was wearing a windbreaker, unzipped, over an ankle length sundress, and a long, streaming scarf. Her hair, which was trying to stay tucked behind her ears, tugged to the side where it had come loose.

She looked happy.

The man next to her was much taller than she was, practically a giant. His arm casually draped around her shoulders. He was remarkably handsome, with a cleft chin and dimples in his smile. The loose locks of his hair had flipped over in the breeze, looking almost comic. Their happiness shined.

Who was he?

She heard a noise from behind her and picked up the bag, dragging it outside with her. "My arms are falling off."

"You can do it!" Ruth cheered.

How the bag made it into the dumpster, Angie didn't know, but finally the heavy lifting was done. She went back inside. Ruth stood in front of her wall of photographs looking thoughtful with one finger laid alongside her cheek.

"How time passes," she said. "Who would have thought, when we were younger, that we would still be here?"

"When you're really young, it seems like nothing will ever change," Angie said.

"That's true. Ach, I remember spending so much time looking in the mirror as a girl, thinking that I would never be as pretty as Ann-Margaret or Farrah Fawcett. That girl, she seems to be so pretty now." She was looking at a picture of three women sitting on the hood of a pale green El Camino: Ruth, Aunt Margery, and Dory, all three of them incredibly young.

"Look at us now. Old and fat."

"And happy?"

"Happiness is fleeting. Don't wish for it. Because the second you ask yourself, 'Am I happy?' the answer has to be no. Strive for satisfaction."

The two of them left the shop, with Ruth locking up behind them. Dory and Aunt Margery were waiting for her in the parking lot, sitting on the hood of Dory's Toyota. Angie had to smile. Definitely in cahoots, she thought.

"Ready?" Dory asked.

"Finally," Aunt Margery added.

"I don't want to hear it! It would have taken longer if I hadn't had someone's help." Ruth slipped an arm around Angie's waist and squeezed.

"I thought you were supposed to be out on a date," Dory said to Angie.

"I got distracted."

Dory turned to Aunt Margery. "That's it, then. If hanging out with Ruth is all it takes to distract her from a date, she's never getting married. She's going to die an old maid, like you."

"I *like* being an old maid," Aunt Margery said.

"Not that again," Ruth said. She strode toward the car, climbed into the back seat without another word, and closed the door firmly behind her.

Angie hoped she would be as lucky in her friendships when she was that age.

She waved them off then called Walter's number. He answered after the second ring.

"Angie?"

"How are you?" she said. "Do you need some company?"

"I could desperately use a distraction."

She suggested they return to Sheldon's for supper. His answer, when it came, was a little disheartening: "I'll have to skip, then."'

"Why? Didn't you like it?"

"I liked it well enough, but my lawyer's asked me to stay away from the public view for a while. He doesn't want any pictures being taken of me."

She thought quickly. "Then I'll pick up something on the way over to the B&B. You said you were staying at Jellicoe House?"

He confirmed and she told him she'd be there as quickly as possible, bearing food and libations.

"And a book," he said.

"What do you want?"

"I don't care. It just has to be good enough to distract me until all this is over."

She wasn't sure that a single book would do the trick, but she would do her best to find the right one.

#

Jellicoe House was a slate-gray building with white trim and windows divided into small, slim panes of glass. Most of the curtains were pulled, but the windows still glowed with warm, reassuring light.

Walter sat on the front porch on the edge of a rocking chair with his hands folded in front of him, head down. He was both wired as tight as a piano string and lost in thought.

Angie drove around the side of the B&B and parked behind the building with the rest of the guests. She had brought the makings for a picnic supper. Jellicoe House didn't overlook the beach, but it was on a small hill and had a decent view of the water in the daytime, if you didn't mind the row of mansions between the B&B and the water.

When she came around the corner, Walter seemed oblivious to her approach. She decided not to startle him. Instead she stood quietly next to him, grocery bags in hand. It was a fresh, cool night, and she was glad that she had put on a jacket before she'd left for the grocery store.

Finally, he looked up at her. "How long have you been standing there?"

"Only a moment or two."

"I'd invite you upstairs, but I can't stand being cooped up inside any longer than I have to be. 'Stay inside during daylight hours.' It's like a prison sentence."

The light had drained from his eyes in the last few days. All Angie wanted to do was help.

"I have a plan," she told him, and handed him the bags of groceries before running into the B&B for a bottle opener and a sharp knife.

Then the two of them headed out for the top of the hill. The small patch of land was owned by the B&B, and held a pair of picnic tables under a single light. She wouldn't exactly have called it romantic, but it would do.

She handed Walter the bottle opener and the Belgian beer, then started setting out the rest of her provisions: salami, pâté, a few cheeses, cornichons, crackers, fig jam, fresh plums.

"All we need now is to be serenaded by a Spanish guitar player while we eat," Walter joked.

She appreciated his effort, but then he fell silent. Angie tried to start a conversation several times, but he kept giving one-word answers. Not a night for witty banter. She tried to give him some silence.

"I'm sorry, I'm terrible company," he said finally. "But I appreciate your coming here and feeding me. I've been eating these amazing B&B breakfasts...then frozen dinners for the other meals. But..."

He went silent again, swallowing several times.

"My mother isn't taking it well," he said. "In fact the reason that I'm at the B&B is that she kicked me out of her house. She says it was all my fault that Father died."

"How on earth could she possibly think that?"

"She says that if I hadn't been here, on the island, he never would have let that burglar into the house."

The lack of logic infuriated Angie, as well as Phyllis's gall to blame her only son. "That makes no sense whatsoever."

"I know. But that's my mom for you."

"What?" said Angie "The burglar was pretending to be you? And what makes her so sure it was a burglar? What did the burglar steal? I'm sorry, Walter, but I think whoever killed your father went over there with the intent to do it."

She hated when she got this way. Her nosy know-it-all self couldn't help but come forth when everyone was dancing around the crime and coming up with half-baked theories instead of really thinking it through.

Walter's eyes seemed to sink deeper into his face.

"I'm sorry, Walter," Angie said. "It's bad enough you have to deal with your father's death. I just feel, well, strangely protective of you."

He nodded and gave her a genuine smile. "I appreciate that."

The wind kicked up white caps in the ocean. They looked like small hands waving at them.

"Did you ever find her that night?" Angie asked.

He looked at her. "I'm not supposed to talk about anything even remotely important, even to you. Lawyer's orders."

A car drove up to the front of the B&B. Angie turned around to look at it. A police cruiser. Walter sighed and finished off the rest of his bottle of beer, then stood up. "I better be going."

"Going?"

"I have a feeling that cop car's for me."

"Why?"

He didn't answer her, only walked back down the hill with his hands in the pockets of his jeans.

The two police officers had gone inside. By the time Walter reached the bottom of the hill, they had come back out again and were walking his way.

They asked him his name and he nodded.

"You're under arrest for the murder of Alexander Snuock. You have the right to remain silent...'

One of the officers padded him down and put handcuffs on him. The other one held open the door as Walter climbed in.

Walter didn't look back at her until he was in the back of the car and the police were turning around in the parking lot. Then he looked at her, and the three of them drove away.

She suddenly felt overexposed on the small hill with the darkening sky as open as a gaping mouth. She wrapped her arms around herself. If she had had to put a word to the expression on his face, it would have been *resigned.*

Chapter 7

YO HO HO AND A BOTTLE OF RUM

She drove back into town feeling lonely and disoriented. She went home and paced the house for a while, then to the bookstore. Aunt Margery had been thorough. There wasn't much she could even pretend to do other than paperwork, and she just wasn't in the mood for that.

She tried to pet Captain Parfait but he shook her off. His ears were back and he was stalking something in the children's book section.

She called Jo, but the call went straight to voice mail. Mickey, on the other hand, had the decency to answer his phone.

"Hypothetically," he said without saying hello, "how would you make a child's Halloween cake in such a way that you wouldn't freak out any children."

Still obsessing about Halloween cakes. Angie shook her head. "No spiders."

"Are you sure about that?"

"Pretty sure."

"Blood?"

"Nope. No blood, either. Skeletons are okay."

"But—"

"Mickey."

"Ahhh, okay." She could practically hear the wind being let out of his sails. "When's the last time you saw Walter?"

"Mickey."

"Is it because he's rich? Is that the attraction?"

"Don't."

"I can't help it."

"Well try." She looked out her storefront window. The street lamps glowed against the dark. Damn Jo and her big mouth. "We're friends, right?"

"Yeah. Friends...You really called for Jo didn't you?"

"I cannot tell a lie. Where is she?"

"At Mom's. Or so she says."

"So she says?"

"She doesn't normally go over to Mom's, even if they were fighting and just made up."

"So she's somewhere else?"

"Who knows. I don't keep tabs on them," he said.

She heard voices in the background. "Where are you?"

"Me? At Sheldon's."

"What are you doing over there?"

"There's some kind of mini-business association meeting going on. In other words, the Snuock renters are over here debating whether they're going to—" He broke off. "It's Angie, that's who." Another pause. "I know we're not supposed to talk about Walter Snuock, but is it true he just got—"

She could hear a shout in the background; another voice shouted back then several others. It sounded as if a riot were about to start.

Over the noise, Mickey shouted, "Angie, can you hear me? I think you better come over and put a couple of minds at ease. As much as you can, anyway."

She heard the sound of breaking glass. Well, whatever else this evening was turning into, at least it wouldn't be lonely.

#

Sheldon nervously greeted her at the door. "Welcome, welcome. So glad to see you. You do know what happened to Walter, don't you?"

"He's been arrested," she said shortly.

"For...the murder of his father?"

"Yes. I was there and heard the officer say that."

Sheldon shook his head then guided her inside. "If you'd say a few words to everyone...you don't happen to know whether Walter's going to keep that cursed rental increase in place?"

"He was so upset when I saw him that I couldn't make myself ask. I don't think he could have answered anyway."

Sheldon patted her on the arm.

The inside of the restaurant was packed with locals; the noise had apparently driven away all the tourists. Angie saw a flash of green hair next to the bar.

"Jo!" she shouted. Mickey was standing next to her. When he spotted Angie looking at him, he pointed to the top of Jo's head and shook his head while mouthing something. Whatever he hoped to get across was lost on her.

Jo put up a finger, knocked back a shot of whiskey, and banged the glass down on the bar. "Another, bartender!"

Nobody was at the bar.

But the gigantic figure of Raymond Quinn was standing in front of it. He towered over everyone else in the room, his gray hair pulled back in a ponytail and his beard spread wildly over his plaid shirt.

"That bastard tried to steal everything from me," Quinn said, too loudly. If Angie had had to guess, she would have said he was a little drunk. "My boats, my women, my dogs, my cigarettes. There wasn't anything of mine that that bastard could leave alone!"

"Hear, hear!" Jo shouted.

As Sheldon brought Angie up to the bar, Jo shouted, "Another, bartender!"

"I think that's enough for the both of you," Sheldon said. "Any more and you'll be setting my chairs on fire again."

Surprisingly, Quinn turned red. "That was an accident."

"You were drunk on purpose though," Sheldon said primly.

Angie looked around for Sheldon's wife, but she was nowhere to be seen, she must have beat a hasty retreat.

Most of the people around here were fishermen and tour boat operators. The rest were shop owners that weren't part of Aunt Margery's set. If the rent increases went through, more than just Jo and Mickey would be hurt.

Sheldon said, "What would you like, my dear?"

She wasn't about to start drinking in this crowd. "A ginger ale, please."

"That's not a real man's drink," Jo announced.

"No hair on my chest, thanks." Angie had to raise her voice to be heard above the rest of the small crowd. "What's up with you tonight? Everything okay?"

Jo stuck out her tongue and blew a raspberry, then beat her hand on the bar top.

Sheldon went around to the other side and poured a pair of ginger ales. Jo tried to knock hers back like whiskey and ended up coughing it out her nose.

Angie sipped hers calmly and watched Raymond Quinn's raucous performance.

"He pushed us all too hard," Quinn was saying. "Even his own son! The reason that Walter murdered his father—"

Sheldon, who had climbed up on a stool behind the bar, put two fingers in his mouth and let out a piercing whistle. "That's enough!"

The room went mostly silent but for the shuffle of feet. Quinn had a defiant look on his face; he opened his mouth, but when Sheldon shot him a hard look he closed it.

"Don't you think it's a little early to start analyzing the motives for a murder when the police haven't announced whether Alexander Snuock was murdered or not yet?" Sheldon glared around the room.

Angie got the feeling that Quinn didn't agree with him, but had realized that he couldn't push Sheldon any further without getting kicked out for the night. Quinn's face was a storm of passing emotions.

"And here we have Miss Angie to tell us exactly what's going on," Sheldon said. "So there's no need to shout about what might have happened...when we have someone who can tell us what actually happened."

Oh, lovely.

Angie said, "I don't know—"

Several people shouted, "I can't hear her!" at the same time. "She's too short!"

Mickey, and Raymond Quinn helped her onto one of the barstools. Wonderful. Just wonderful. She put her hand on Quinn's shoulder to help her balance. Mickey was taller, but Quinn was definitely sturdier.

Everyone looked at her.

She cleared her throat. "I don't know much."

"Tell us what you do know," Jo said.

"Walter has been arrested," she said. Before they could all start talking again, she added, "He didn't say anything about the rent. I didn't have a chance to ask."

"Are you dating him?"

Jo wasn't the one who asked, but her eyes twinkled with the most mischief.

"We went on a date here once and I've fed him twice since then, but I wouldn't call them *dates*," Angie said.

"So you're dating him."

She sighed. "Not exclusively."

"Who else are you dating?"

"Nobody!"

She was starting to lose her temper.

"How long have you known him?"

"Since kindergarten!"

The room erupted in an uproar. She climbed down off the stool and sat on it, and drank her ginger ale with a mixture of angry humiliation.

The crowd seemed to have settled a little. Even though she hadn't been able to tell them much, they seemed relieved. They broke up into smaller groups and drifted away from the bar, back to their tables.

Sheldon had climbed down, too. He leaned forward across the bar, standing on tiptoe: "Thanks, Angie."

"I didn't do anything."

He patted her hand. Raymond Quinn stood up from his stool and said, "Alexander Snuock deserved to die, and you all know it. The man wasn't part of the community. He could do nothing but take, and take, and take. The only reason he hasn't taken everything away from all of us is that he hadn't found a way to do it."

Sheldon said, "You'd best lower your voice, Raymond, or you'll have to take yourself out of the bar."

"Oh, I'm taking myself out of the bar all right," Quinn said. "No need to worry about that. But you can't take the truth out of the bar. Snuock deserved to die. End of story."

He picked up his empty glass and tried to drink out of it, then set it down with dignity and walked out the door.

The men at the tables exchanged serious looks.

Sheldon said, "All right, last call. And I'm serious about this."

After Quinn's comments, no one seemed interested in another drink. The room cleared quickly as Sheldon ran credit cards.

Angie, Jo, and Mickey bussed tables. All three of them had worked in restaurants around the island during their teen years and knew what to do. In a few minutes they had the dining room cleared. Sheldon sat down at one of the booths with his legs stuck out in front of him. "What a night."

The three of them walked out to the parking lot; it had rained, briefly, while they were inside.

"If the police weren't sure that it was murder, then they wouldn't have arrested Walter for it," Angie said.

Jo said, "They must have changed their minds since yesterday."

"What was up with you tonight anyway?" asked Angie.

Jo chose to ignore the question. "You know, when they found him, there was just him and a gun in the room. What were they supposed to think, but that it was suicide? Only I heard that the forensics chick convinced them that the angle was wrong and that he probably hadn't shot himself."

"Were there powder burns?" Mickey asked.

"I didn't hear."

"Jo," Angie said. "Don't try to distract me with clues. This is more important. Are you okay? Why haven't you been answering your phone?"

Jo brushed a hand across the top of her car then sat on the hood. "I found out something else that was pretty spectacular."

"Jo."

"I wasn't with my mother on Thursday night," Jo said. "Okay? I knew that you figured it out. Mom couldn't keep her story straight...she said that Ruth bugged her about it and realized that you must have figured it out."

"Where *were* you?" Angie asked.

"With someone."

"Who?"

"Just...someone," Jo said, running her hands through her hair. "A tourist, okay? It was a one-night stand."

"Wow. Uh..."

"I got his name, I'm just not telling it to you. It's not going to be a thing, all right? So don't start carving my name on trees with someone I've only seen once. And don't blame Mom. She was trying to cover up for me."

"Why didn't you tell me?"

"Because..." Jo clacked her jaws shut. "I was embarrassed."

Angie said, "You're my best friend."

Mickey said, "All right. I'll get out of here so you can do the girl talk thing."

"Thanks, Mickey," Angie said.

"No problem. In fact, you don't even need to consider it a favor." He climbed in his car and took off.

Angie sat on the car hood next to her friend. Jo leaned against her shoulder.

"Dating," Angie said. "What fun."

"I know, right?"

"Wanna tell me about it?" Angie asked.

"You first."

"It wasn't much of an adventure," Angie warned her. "He was too upset." She started telling Jo about her picnic with Walter that ended with him in the back of a police cruiser.

"And he just went with them?" Jo interrupted. "Like that? As they pulled up?"

"Yes. It was like he was expecting it."

"I don't know what that means, but it doesn't make him look innocent," Jo said.

"I guess not. On the other hand, he seemed too washed out and exhausted to look guilty."

"I don't know," Jo said, giving Angie a wry look. "Feeling guilty can really wear you out."

Angie took that as a hint that she was ready to talk. "Tell me all about it."

Jo sighed. "It seems like such a cliché. The woman with the bright green hair and the punk with the mohawk."

They had met down on the beach that afternoon, while Angie had been delivering books to Snuock's mansion on the other side of the island. The two of them had gone to Sheldon's, and had left just before Angie and Walter had arrived, then they'd gone to Jo's apartment.

"Did he spend the night?"

"No," Jo said. "He stayed pretty late, but...he had to go. He had to get back to Boston before noon."

"How late did he *stay*?"

"Five a.m."

Angie rolled her eyes. "Then he stayed all night."

"We were just listening to old records most of the time..." Jo lay back against the windshield. "You know, I used to be pretty wild."

" I know." Angie chuckled.

"But this is the first time that I've done anything like this."

"Do you have his number?"

"I do, but I'm not going to call him."

"Not even to text him?"

"Not while he's at work!"

Angie leaned back so she was beside Jo, the two of them looked at the stars above the streetlights. "Love," she said.

"I'm not in love," said Jo.

"I'm not either...I'm just thinking about it."

"Oh. What?"

"That it's been a long time since I felt anything even remotely romantic for anyone."

"Since your unmentionable ex. You like Walter?"

"I do." It felt good to admit it to Jo.

They kept their eyes on the night sky. A satellite passed overhead.

Chapter 8

OFF THE BOOKS

Angie still had the books that she had selected for Walter in the back of her car. She had no idea whether the police would let her give them to Walter or not, but the decent thing to do seemed to be to ask.

She made it through the bookstore's morning shift in a somewhat groggy mood. She'd tried to force herself to go to bed early, but hadn't been able to sleep; she'd turned to reading her namesake Agatha. She'd already read *Murder on the Orient Express* a dozen times or more; she found one of her dog-eared copies and dragged it, and a cup of warm milk, up to bed with her, hoping that it would put her to sleep.

Jo was hung over, muttering to herself, as she delivered the morning pastries on her bike.

"Did he call?" Angie asked.

"No. And no texts, either."

"Did *you* call?"

"Shut up."

But the words were delivered with a hug. Jo's green hair and Misfits T-shirt made for a surprisingly romantic picture as she pedaled off with her bicycle baskets full of bread into the morning fog between the rows of brick storefronts.

The morning was busy. Angie set up the coffee as she had earlier, with a small sign and a cup for cash, so she could focus on knocking down the espresso drink orders. Pastries flew off the shelves. At nine, Mickey arrived to restock her case.

People lingered in the café area, reading newspapers and books. She had scattered the tables with a selection of classic popular fiction in the smallest mass-market paperback formats, along with a few newspapers. The newspapers were picked apart into sections and traded amongst the patrons, but many of the paperbacks were purchased after the coffee was finished.

Aha.

One of her customers said something that stuck with her: "It's just the right amount of noise in here," she said. "The business of you making coffee, soft guitar music in the background, soft chatter...not like a chain restaurant where you can't hear yourself think, and not like a library where you're afraid to say boo!"

Angie had picked out the music this morning because she'd been feeling nostalgic for something that hadn't happened yet—was there a word for that?—that was, more time with Walter. This time with the Spanish guitar music he had mentioned.

The patrons liked it. She'd have to remember it.

As she worked, her mind wandered. Making lattes didn't occupy too much of her thoughts after having made so many, even when she had a complex half-caff-soy-milk-extra-hot-just-a-dash-of-vanilla-no-sugar order on her hands.

What could she do to help the twins with their bakery rent?

She could give them money to help them stay afloat; maybe that suggestion would sound better coming from her than from their mother.

She could try to drum up more business for them using the bookstore. In between customers, she took the Nantucket Bakery business card from the far side of the counter and put it next to the register, then pulled out a few of the cards and scattered them along the front of the case, in front of the Danishes.

What else?

The cake that Mickey had been making had been pretty clever, she had to admit, yet it was probably too time-consuming to make the centerpiece of their business. Making six hundred blueberry-sage scones was far more cost and time effective than making a single cake; although, if Mickey had to make nothing but scones all day, he would have thrown his apron on the floor and walked out. He was the artist in that family, where Jo was more focused on the business side.

Angie continued through the morning, serving coffee, selling books, and making notes as she went. She didn't come up with any brilliant solutions, just a few ideas she wanted to make sure Jo was tackling. Did she have ads in the local free papers? Was she making sure her customers all had business cards out? What about a radio ad? In Angie's experience, radio almost always was more useful than TV for advertising. But of course it was always so hard to know. Had the local paper been invited to tour the bakery? What kind of website did they have? Did they have a press kit available?

There were a hundred little things that they could and should do before they started paying for advertising, so that when people did see their advertising, all the details—like what services they offered and for how much—would be in place.

The bakery occupied her thoughts until Aunt Margery arrived at eleven.

"Hello, my darling Agnes," she said, kissing Angie on the cheek.

"Good morning, Auntie."

Aunt Margery made a face but didn't complain. "I'm sorry to hear about Walter."

The two of them left it at that while Aunt Margery went over the café supplies and made a list of what she needed Angie to pick up while she was out. Then she checked the catalogues and marked a few titles that she wanted to pick up for the store. Finally, she took over the stool behind the counter. "Tell me about our vacation in Greece in January."

"It might be—"

Aunt Margery raised one hand to cut her off. "Speak to me of dreams, child, not of rent and taxes and such."

Angie laughed and told her about the places they would go: Athens, Crete, the small islands where sea turtles would climb out of the water to lay their eggs on the sand next to your boat and the mermaids who would follow you through the water, singing songs to try to wreck you against the rocks.

Aunt Margery sighed. "A little romance in one's life, that's all one needs in order to survive the vicissitudes of the fates."

"Is that a quote?" Angie asked.

"It's a poetic kind of morning."

It was a minute until noon.

"Now that I'm fortified," said Aunt Margery, "tell me what happened with Walter."

"I thought you knew already."

"As you know, it's one thing to be apprised of the general situation by one's friends, and another thing entirely to hear the details from the horse's mouth. And you, my darling grandniece, will carry me on your strong back as you tell me the tale."

"You *are* in a poetic mood this morning."

"It's afternoon," Aunt Margery corrected her pedantically.

Angie laughed and told her a detailed version of what had happened with Walter, stopping only to help a customer find books on woodworking—she bought all six of the ones that Angie had.

When she had finished, Aunt Margery said, "Yes, you should try to take the books to Walter. I don't know that they'll give them to him, but it shouldn't hurt to try. If not, they can just say no."

"I wonder what they'll do with his luggage at Jellicoe House."

"I'll call and make sure they don't do anything odd with it," Aunt Margery said. "They'll have to rent out the room again, unless he's paid in advance, but it shouldn't be a problem."

"You know he has a lawyer." Angie said.

"Being a Snuock and having gone to law school himself, I would imagine so, although I hope he has hired a specialist to help defend him if it goes to trial."

Angie shuddered.

"It's something you'll have to think about," Aunt Margery said. "What position you would like to be in, if it should."

"I don't think he's the murderer, Aunt Margery."

"I didn't say he was...but until this gets resolved, one way or another, you're a suspect. At the very least, no matter what happens, you'll have to be a witness during the trial."

Angie thought about going on the stand and being asked the same kind of repetitive questions that the detectives had asked her, going on and on for hours—it gave her a sense of perspective about all the mystery novels that she had ever read. She had always sneered at witnesses who lied on the stand and got caught—surely she, Angie, would have been able to keep her story together.

But now she wasn't so sure. The questioning had been mentally exhausting. At least if she were called up to the witness stand she wouldn't have to lie about anything, unless Walter really *was* guilty of murdering his father.

Would she lie then?

She made a face.

"Think about what you would like to have happen," Aunt Margery repeated. "Before it's too late."

#

After picking up everything Aunt Margery needed and dropping it off, Angie drove to the police station, a red brick building with white columns in front of the entrance on the east end of town, with her small stack of books.

The receptionist at the front desk frowned at her. "Ma'am, I can't allow you to give those books to him personally. You'll need to get approval from the supervising officer on duty, and Clarkeson's busy right now."

"Can I leave them with you? They're just books."

"New books?"

Angie went through the stack. "One used book."

"Usually people want to bring clothes...and the clothes have to be new. I'd forget about the used book just in case."

Angie pulled it out. The receptionist eyeballed the rest of the stack. Angie had pulled out five good history books, not on the Russians but on the Ottoman Empire, just for variety. They had been books that Alexander Snuock had enjoyed, but she didn't plan to tell Walter that.

Sometimes it was upsetting, finding out how similar you were to your parents.

Angie gave the receptionist a hopeful look. The man sighed.

"I'll try," he said. "I can't guarantee anything, but I'll try."

He stood up and slid the books off the top of his desk, and put them on a shelf in the back of the room, along with a scribbled tag that he stuck between the pages of the top book.

When he saw that Angie was still standing there, he said, "Anything else?" in a put-upon tone.

"I'd like to visit him, if I may."

The receptionist said, "I have some paperwork for you to fill out," and slid over a form.

Forty-five minutes later, Angie had surrendered her purse, keys, and belt, and was sitting on the other side of a heavy plexiglass window with guards standing on the other side of the room. Walter wore what looked like a set of bright orange nursing scrubs.

"Hi," she said.

"Thanks for coming," he said. "You know who hasn't visited me? My mother."

For a moment, it sounded like he was in a pretty negative mood. Then he laughed.

"Sorry. It just struck me as ironic, but not surprising. Someone I've known for only a few days is more thoughtful than the woman who gave birth to me. I love her, and there are a lot of things I love *about* her, but I've never understood her, and I've never seen what Dad used to see in her."

"You haven't known me a few days," Angie said. "You've known me since kindergarten."

"True, but non-continuously since seventh grade, Ms. Smarty-pants. I don't think that counts." He took several deep breaths. I know why you're here."

"Oh?"

"You thought to yourself, Walter was such a snob, he would barely talk to me the other night...and yet, for the honor of the bookselling profession, I must still deliver the book he asked for," he said, teasingly. Then he quickly switched to a serious tone, "Do you have it?"

She felt her face go a little red. "The officer on duty has to approve them. I left them at the front desk. They don't let you bring this stuff in with you."

"You might be passing me escape plans and files to cut through the bars."

"I might be passing you razor blades and meth along the spines," she said.

"Ah, good point. Okay, that's reasonable. What did you bring?"

"I've already given you my best Russian nonfiction, so I decided to go with the Ottomans. They and the Russians were so often in conflict that I thought you might like to get the rest of the story."

"Are these ones that you picked out for my father?"

Now she was *definitely* blushing. "Maybe."

He laughed. "Sometimes you're more predictable than you think."

She tossed her hair back over her shoulder. "But what books did I bring? Tell me that!"

"That's the fun part of the surprise. Don't tell me. I'll just look forward to them. When I get them, eventually."

They looked at each other. She didn't know what else to say. She didn't know him well enough to say the things that might actually help him feel better; she didn't know what landmines to avoid so he wouldn't feel worse.

"I didn't kill my father," Walter said suddenly.

Angie nodded.

"You believe me?"

"Why wouldn't I believe you?"

"Because I'm the logical suspect."

"You don't seem guilty to me."

"What if it was an accident, and I don't feel guilty because it wasn't something that I intended?"

She suddenly felt like she was on a high-wire and trying desperately not to look down. "That sort of sounds like an admission of guilt." She took a breath. "But had you accidentally killed your dad, from what I know of you, you wouldn't have been able to cover it up without revealing yourself in the process."

"Really?"

"You kind of wear your heart on your sleeve."

"I'm easy to read? Coming from you..." He laughed. "*You're* easy to read. You look so frightened right now."

She gave him a hesitant smile, "You're sending some strange messages."

"I know." He interlaced his fingers and rested them in front of him. "Boy does it make you squirm."

"Your father liked to see me squirm,"

That did it, now his face was flat. "I'm sorry. I don't like to seem like him."

She shook her head. "We both belong to families that have been on the island for a long time. We're kind of genetically predictable."

"It's family destiny, then?"

"Probably it's more complicated than that. But it's pretty easy to interpret a book that you've been reading for generations. Or something like that."

They chatted about books and family for a few moments, coming to agree that new generations of a family were like the latest sequel in a long-running series, and that by-blows were like spin-off series.

Angie didn't know how he was surviving the sterility of the prison—all metal and white linoleum, hard and odorless—but she was glad to see he was in good humor despite everything.

Finally Walter sighed and said, "I only have a few minutes left before my time's up... I think my father's murder was an accident. I just don't know whose accident it was."

"Your mom's?" she knew it was an invasive question, but it had to be asked.

He took a second. "I don't think she had anything to do with my father's death. Just..." His shoulders fell. "It's so complicated."

"Do you have an alibi for the fourth? Surely someone must have seen you when you went out looking for your mother."

"Not for the fourth."

One of the guards called out, "Time."

Walter stood up. He leaned into the plexiglass.

"Did my father pay you for those books?"

"Please, don't worry about it."

"Send me a bill."

"Walter, this isn't the time to discuss bills. It's the least I can do."

The guard shifted from foot to foot. "Time!"

Walter turned his head, "Just one minute." Then back to Angie. "Listen. They'll figure out that I didn't do it eventually. From some of the questions that they've been asking me, it sounds like he was killed on the night of the third, not the fourth. And I was with you."

The guard was at his back, tapping him on the shoulder.

Walter gave Angie a quick but reassuring smile then turned and was ushered back through the heavy armored door. Her chest fluttered. The *third*, not the fourth! That changed everything. Walter had an alibi. Her. The question now was, who didn't have an alibi on the third?

#

She spent a few hours wandering aimlessly along the children's beach, watching the children play and reading a book on her phone. She didn't feel like eating but made herself stop at a fast-food restaurant for a quick meal.

It felt like she was being tortured by her own thoughts, which swirled around in her head endlessly. The same scenes over and over again: the sight of Alexander Snuock's body, the scenes leading up to his discovery. Sobbing in the kitchen. *I should have gone back up to see the body again, when I was calmer.* Her date with Walter at Sheldon's Shuckery—everyone had seen the two of them together, but then everyone knew when they had left, too, and after that, there hadn't been much of a chance of a witness providing an alibi for Walter. It would all depend on the time of death.

She returned to the bookstore in time to help Aunt Margery close, gave her a brief description of the visit, and opened up the bookstore financial reports on her computer, and calculated a few test profit-and-loss sheets for the bookstore based on last year's sales, next year's projected sales, and the new rental rates.

The good news was that this year's sales had been better than last year's sales. The bad news was that she didn't think there would be enough money to take the trip to Greece in January.

She ran the numbers for closing the shop in January, but without the vacation to Greece, and those looked better. She could do one or the other: close the shop or take the vacation to Greece. But not both.

Soon it was midnight and of course Aunt Margery had gone. Angie vaguely remembered a kiss on the cheek, but couldn't recall when. Captain Parfait had head-butted her leg a few times, too. She glanced around the back room, then stuck her head out the door—he was in his basket by the window, sound asleep.

When you've stayed awake later than your cat...

She went back to the books. In short, she had to admit that Snuock had been right. She had a clear margin of safety; she wouldn't lose the bookstore. That was what she had to focus on, not the lost vacation. *She wasn't being put out of business.*

Snuock's ghost would be happy if Quinn were put out of business, of course. But what about everyone else? Snuock's ghost could probably care less. He'd grown up on this island and had relationships with hundreds of people on it, not least of which were the ones with his tenants.

Why was one enmity more important to him than hundreds of other amicable relationships? Was there more to it than Aunt Margery and her friends had implied? Quinn seemed to think so—that Snuock had been trying to steal everything from him for decades.

But what had been the driving force on Snuock's part?

What made him treat the sacrifice of so much goodwill in the community as worthwhile? What had made it a reasonably good bargain?

Eventually, she closed up her accounting program and wandered aimlessly through the bookshelves, waking Captain Parfait and making him follow her all around the store. He probably didn't think much of her hunting ability. If she were tracking a mouse, he wanted to be in on the kill.

And the change in the timeline from the fourth of July to the third... what effect did that have? She didn't know where Quinn had been either night. She suspected him. Who didn't? The only reason that he hadn't been arrested was that they were currently laying the blame on Walter.

If Quinn had done it, and she could prove it...that would solve all her problems in one neat bow. Because if it hadn't been Quinn, and she was sure that it wasn't Walter, who else could it have been?

Cui bono? Who benefits?

She, Angie, would have benefited from Snuock's death. So would the rest of the business owners. Would anyone else? Anyone could have made it onto the island in the last few days; the streets were crawling with tourists. Pay cash, take a ferry, and carry out the revenge that you've always dreamed of...

A business deal gone sour, a former romantic entanglement with a grudge, a former employee who had gone postal. There had to be a thousand people with a motive to harm Snuock, people for whom he trusted enough to open the gate.

But whom *did* he trust enough to let onto his property while everyone else was out?

Conversely...whom did he hate enough to let onto his property while everyone else was out?

The three main people she could think of whose businesses were at risk were Quinn...and of course the twins.

Snuock hated Quinn enough. But the twins? He only knew them as tenants. He'd mentioned wanting to manipulate them, sure, but that wasn't hate. That was just Snuock's standard business operating procedures.

Jo hadn't been at her mother's house that night, but the story about the tourist with the mohawk (if completely believable to Angie) wasn't something that the cops could check out, probably. No, wait. She'd said that she had the guy's phone number. If she really had the guy's phone number, then she could give that to the police and they could call the guy and confirm the story.

So Jo should be safe.

Mickey? He'd said something about what he'd been doing that night. Working on that weird Halloween cake? Unless someone had seen the lights on at the bakery and looked in the window, he wouldn't have an alibi. The fact that his car would have been parked behind the bakery wasn't enough to prove that he was at the bakery. But wouldn't the police have to have some kind of evidence putting him at the scene of the crime? They couldn't just arrest him for renting from Snuock, could they? And if they could, wouldn't they just arrest Quinn first?

The suspects as they stood: Walter, Quinn, and Mickey. Quinn being the most likely of the three.

And wasn't it true that the most obvious solution was usually the true one?

Chapter 9

THE PIRATE

The little house was quiet when Angie finally returned, the kind of quiet that made her think that her great-aunt had gone out to the beach to wait for her pirate lover and watch the waves roll in. She felt tired, but knew that she wasn't going to be able to sleep, so she made a small pot of tea that she poured into two insulated travel mugs, wrapped herself up in an ancient picnic blanket, and walked down the quiet street.

The last few days had been stressful, to say the least. The night was quiet. A few horns echoed in the distance, the flashing light from the lighthouse kept time with her footsteps. Most of the dogs had been taken inside for the night and most of the seagulls had found a roost, although she could hear a few dogs and birds in the distance.

She smelled the scent of a fire and wondered whether anyone had started one. The police tended to look the other way unless a rowdy party was involved. A quiet fire, far away from anything that could burn, was one of the necessary pleasures of living on an island like this. If you had to give up some of the conveniences of living on the mainland, at least you should be able to sit by the waterside, your eyes shifting between the rushing waves and the flickering flames, and reclaim some of your soul.

It was one of the reasons that she had come back. The other was family. Not her parents, strangely. She loved them, but even before she had come back they were up and roaming. It was the solidity of Aunt Margery and her friends that had called to her. Also, the feeling that she had something similar in her friendships with Jo and Mickey: through thick and thin. After her broken romance with her ex, she figured out what was most important to her—friendship and loyalty.

She had taken the long way to the beach in order to give her more time with her thoughts, but hadn't thought of what it meant to walk with a blanket over her shoulders and a pair of sealed travel mugs in her hands. In short, the arrangement was too awkward for her to be able to put anything down and open a lid so she could drink tea while she walked. When she spotted the small bonfire on the beach she was glad to see it. She would hand Aunt Margery her mug, spread out the blanket, and drink her tea.

Then she saw the silhouettes moving next to it and stopped just past the concrete dividers at the end of the parking lot.

One of the silhouettes was Aunt Margery: short, round in the belly, a particularly rounded kind of walking. The other one was huge. Immense. Broad shoulders and slashing hand gestures.

Raymond Quinn.

The two of them argued by the fire, and stood closer together than they might have if they were only casual acquaintances.

Angie watched them. She couldn't hear everything they said, but snatches of their words carried up to her, almost preternaturally, as if she were watching a stage play from the back row.

"Leave her alone," her great-aunt snapped angrily.

"I'll do what I please."

"You always have, you great idiot. You've hurt more people than I can count doing it. You do what you like, though! That's..." And then she muttered something that Angie couldn't catch.

"I'll do what I please," Quinn repeated stubbornly.

"You're only doing it to spite Snuock, and he's dead!"

Those words echoed clearly. Angie didn't dare move.

Quinn muttered something too quietly for Angie to hear.

Aunt Margery turned toward the flames and poked them angrily with a thick branch of driftwood. "And then what? He's just a boy, Quinn."

"Oh please."

"*And* you're sleeping with his mother."

"Snuock's taint hasn't been on her for decades," Quinn said. "He doesn't own her. And now what can he do to her, from beyond the grave?"

"But will you still feel that way when her alimony is cut off?"

Quinn answered softly with a question that Angie didn't catch.

Aunt Margery snapped, "Yes, her alimony! Her big fat allowance! Or do you think that Snuock didn't write a letter to his lawyers the day he suspected that the two of you were involved, stating that if anything should happen to him, Phyllis would be cut off from all funds?"

Quinn shook his head angrily.

Angie was dizzy with these new facts spinning in her mind. Phyllis Snuock had been sleeping with Raymond Quinn. Quinn was the lover? It made perfect sense to Angie now. The rent increase was a direct result of Quinn's relationship with Phyllis. Walter had complained about trying to go between his parents, lest his father cut off his mother's and his own funds. If this was the reason why, no wonder he was stressed. Snuock must have been furious.

Quinn had killed Snuock and set it up so that Walter would be blamed. And didn't give a damn that the son of the woman he was seeing would take responsibility for a murder he had committed...

Angie was horrified. She had wanted, almost wished, to find out that Quinn was the murderer, but—this was too much.

How long had the affair been going on, anyway? Whose son was Walter? He *was* taller than his father had been...but so was Phyllis. If he were Quinn's son then Quinn was just as cold-hearted as Snuock, unless he didn't know that Walter was his son.

Suddenly she noticed that Quinn was walking straight at her, storming away from the bonfire. Angie suppressed a yelp and backed away slowly, trying to keep a parked car between him and a clear view of her. Should she duck down?

One of the streetlights lit up Quinn's face. *The streetlights.* As long as she didn't put one of the lights to her back, he shouldn't be able to pick her out.

She was lucky. Quinn didn't see her, either because he was too involved with his own thoughts, or because she managed to stay crouched down in the shadows.

Once he passed her, she turned tail and fled in the opposite direction, barely noticing where her feet took her.

The next thing she knew—still wrapped in a blanket and clutching her mugs of tea—she was on the road to the lighthouse on Brandt Point, flashing its light in the darkness, with mansions to the left and right. Fortunately, the tide was out. She walked onto the beach, sat on her blanket, and stared at the waves for an hour, then got up to head back home.

She took the longer way back so that she could look down at the children's beach and see whether her aunt was still there. The fire had been put out.

Angie put the two travel mugs on the concrete dividers, took the old picnic blanket off her shoulders and folded it over the other side of the divider. The night had grown much cooler, and she shivered before stepping onto the sand.

Where she had seen the bonfire earlier, there was nothing but burnt wood and ashes. Aunt Margery was nowhere to be seen. For a moment, Angie thought about calling out her name. But of course she'd only gone home. She was perfectly safe and sound.

Nevertheless, Angie looked across the beach for any suspicious shapes in the darkness. The night was a dark one, with clouds covering the sky, and she couldn't make out much. Every time her eyes fastened on movement, it was a small bird wading in the shallows, or a wave that didn't crash on the shore quite like the ones around it.

No bodies.

She closed her eyes and listened to the waves come in for a few minutes. It normally calmed her, but tonight it was only making her feel more tense. It felt like something was coming up behind her, the hairs on the back of her neck stood on end.

Quinn had been angry at her great-aunt. It had felt like a threat. She had to make sure that he hadn't done something to her.

Had they been friends, once upon a time?

Someone had kicked sand over the fire to put it out; the ashes were still warm. Angie stood next to it to soak up what little heat was left. Go home and sleep or stay up all night? It had been ages since she'd done that. She needed a break. The days were starting to bleed together; she was that tired.

Cupcakes.

Ideas came at the most bizarre moments. That's what the twins needed to do. Cupcakes.

Angie had seen dozens of custom cupcake places out in Manhattan, but nobody on the island had caught up with the trend. She should talk to Mickey about them tomorrow. Something simple. He could make her a half-dozen cupcakes with tiny fondant books on top; a miniature teacup; the tiniest of strawberries; a cupcake with a cupcake on top. He wouldn't have to make the *same* cupcakes, either. In fact it would be better if he didn't.

She picked up a stick from inside the fire and used it to doodle a picture of a cupcake with a tiny book on top. The stick snapped before she had finished. She reached for another one; this one tugged something along with it from the ashes.

A piece of cloth.

Strange. She pulled it out of the ashes. It was a piece of flowery fabric that had partially melted—definitely not cotton or silk. A blouse? A dress? She tried to use the stick to spread out the sandy, twisted piece, then knelt on the sand and used her hands. It was a dress, a floral paisley one, with a single ruffle along the neckline, and...spaghetti straps.

One of Aunt Margery's much regretted fashion mistakes? One of Phyllis's old dresses, tossed away by Quinn? Where had Phyllis been, on the night of the third? Something tugged at Angie's mind. Had she seen this dress before?

#

Angie kicked over the remains of the bonfire and scraped through them with a stick. She found a charred piece of cloth, but they were almost completely burnt away. She bit her lip. Either she wasn't going to do this at all, or she was going to do it right.

She broke up the burnt branches and tossed them in a garbage can, then kicked the ashes of the fire so that the sand wouldn't clump together. The tide was rolling in, and the waterline was almost to the edge of the fire. It all would be washed away by morning.

She lay the picnic blanket out on the sand, sat on it for a few minutes and drank both her tea and Aunt Margery's. Then she got up, shook out the sand as best she could, and put the dress in the center.

She could think of a thousand ways that this could go wrong. She was leaving physical evidence behind as well as acting suspiciously. There were a number of houses overlooking the beach.

How many people were still awake? How many people had seen her?

She didn't dare to check her phone to find out the time. The lit phone screen would just be a tiny beacon saying, "Look at me, look at me!"

She added the travel mugs to the bundle and wrapped it up in a compact package. She was trembling. Even if someone stopped to talk to her (at dark o'clock in the morning), the clothing was hidden well enough in the blanket that it wouldn't be seen.

She crossed her fingers and started walking back.

The wind had died down and it was quiet. Even the random fireworks explosions that had been going off for the last week had stopped.

Please let everyone be asleep.

#

Angie made a point to kick off her sandy shoes outside the back door. Next to them was a pair of Aunt Margery's sandals.

Would she be up or wouldn't she?

Angie remembered one of the few times that she'd stayed out later than she'd realized as a teenager. She'd come home to find her parents both sound asleep and had been deeply, deeply shocked. She could have *died* for all they knew—she could have been dead for hours before they'd found out. Her heart had raced.

Jo and Mickey would have given their left eyes for a mother that would have hounded them less than Dory did. But then Dory had had her twins later in life and had treated them like her precious diamonds, treasure that had to be protected from the thieves and con artists of the world. The fact that her daughter, especially, could be one of those con artists seemed to be lost on her. In fact, it had been Jo that Angie had been out with that night when she'd come home so late.

In the morning, Angie's mother had said, "Everything go all right last night?"

Angie broke. If she had any intention of lying to her parents, her willpower snapped at the first sleepy pre-coffee yawn.

"I'm so sorry! I was having fun at a party and I forgot—"

Her mother pulled her daughter in and kissed her on the head. "Everyone has to have adventures sometime," she said. "Just remember, don't drink anything that you didn't pour yourself. Never take any drugs that you didn't buy."

"Mom!"

Her mother made an evil chuckle. "We weren't worried. We knew you were with Mickey and Jo."

Angie's eyes had bulged. "But—"

They were the ones who had helped her get in trouble.

Her mother said, "Just imagine if someone tried to take advantage of you when either of *them* were around."

Her father, who had yet to say a word, snorted into his coffee and walked off with the newspaper.

Aunt Margery, on the other hand, had *words* with Angie the next morning. She'd always compensated for Angie's parents' carefree discipline by reminding her that the world was not so forgiving.

Angie took a deep breath, fumbled for her keys, and unlocked the back door. Awkwardly, she let herself in while trying to wipe the last of the sand off the bottoms of her feet.

The lights were off in the kitchen, but...she knew that Aunt Margery was awake. How Angie knew, she didn't know. But the whole house felt expectant.

She yawned so hard that her jaws creaked then she put the blanket carefully in the sink, taking the two travel mugs out and leaving them on the side. She walked through the tiny door to the utility room and put the blanket into the dirty-clothes basket.

What to do with the burnt dress?

She took off her sandy pants and socks, dumped them in the wash and started it. With the rush of water to help cover any delays or unexpected sounds, she pulled a heavy freezer bag out of its box on the shelves next to the door and put the burnt clothing scraps inside. She picked out as much as she could, leaving only ash behind. Then she put the blanket in the wash and dropped the lid.

She checked her hands for soot, opened the lid of their tiny stand-alone freezer, pulled out a bag of frozen burritos, and dropped the clothing under the bag of burritos. After a moment, she took two of the burritos out of the bag.

Yawning, she walked back into the dark kitchen. A dark silhouette stood in the doorway.

Angie startled, slapping her hand to her chest.

Aunt Margery.

"What are you doing putting laundry on before sunrise?" said Aunt Margery.

"You shouldn't lurk in dark doorways." Angie could feel her pulse racing. "I tried to find you out on the beach and bring you some tea so we could watch for pirates together...but you were busy. So I doubled back and went out by the lighthouse instead."

Aunt Margery sighed. "You saw him."

"Yup. How long has that been going on?"

"There is no *that*," her great-aunt snapped. "Or at least, there hasn't been any *that* since high school."

Whao. Angie had been referring to Phyllis, but Aunt Margery was talking about herself. "Raymond Quinn is your *pirate*?"

"He was, once upon a time," Aunt Margery said. "But then I realized that he drank and smoked too much, didn't bathe often enough, and was never going to do anything but complain about how the Alexander Snuocks of the world didn't deserve what they had. So I decided that I'd rather have a dream pirate instead."

"That's fair and quite imaginative," Angie said, admiring her aunt's resourcefulness. She carried the burritos over to the counter and prepped them on a plate, then stuck them in the microwave. "Hungry?"

"No, thank you."

"So how did he know to find you...oh...that's where you used to meet him, wasn't it? On the beach?"

"Yes."

"Is he the reason that you never fell in love again?"

Aunt Margery twisted her face into a doubtful expression. "Who's to say I didn't?"

"Scandalous," Angie said. She yawned again. She couldn't let her aunt know that she knew about Phyllis and Quinn. If it got back to Quinn it would make Angie a liability. "I would actually love to hear all about it, but tomorrow's going to be a pain. I don't know how you do it, staying up so late."

"I have a great-niece who gets up early and handles all the annoying morning things," Aunt Margery said. "Oh, you should have seen him."

"Who?"

"Ray. He was quite handsome, back in the day—the very picture of tall, dark, and handsome. He shaved his beard back then, and we were all in love with his dimples...shame that he's turned out so bitter. Otherwise he would have made someone a good husband."

Angie wondered what Quinn would have said about Aunt Margery: "Shame she was so clever...she might have made me a good wife if she'd been a little less shrewish."

Something like that, she thought. She yawned again and said goodnight.

#

Angie caught a few hours of sleep before her alarm went off. She pressed snooze once, then bounced out of bed—she had to move the freezer bag full of clothes!

Aunt Margery's room was downstairs, and the floors creaked. Her great-aunt had *sworn* that she could sleep through a herd of elephants running around upstairs and not to worry about early-morning creaks, but the last thing Angie wanted to do was wake her.

But it was hard not to run straight downstairs.

Once Angie had the coffee brewing, she checked the laundry. The sand had washed out of the blanket and jeans and socks, no hidden pockets of granular sludge in the pockets or anything. It looked like a gray, damp sort of morning outside, so she put everything in the dryer and left a note in front of the coffeemaker: "Please check blanket in dryer isn't damp."

Then, finally, she allowed herself a chance to look in the freezer.

The bag with the dress looked undisturbed.

She had to move it—she and her great-aunt pulled things out of the freezer or put things into it every other day, it seemed like. She put it on a shelf and lowered the washer's lid quietly.

She filled a travel mug with coffee, turned off the coffee pot and made sure the main lid was sealed (it was insulated and would still be hot by the time Aunt Margery woke up). She popped open the refrigerator door, took out the big container of cream, poured a teacup half full of it, put that back in the refrigerator, and put the carton in a noisy, rustling plastic bag.

She added another note to the one on the counter: "P.S., took cream, can't remember if enough at P&P, will pick up more later, cream in cup in fridge."

Then she put the bag of burnt clothing in with the carton of cream, grabbed her keys and phone, and left for work.

Was she going overboard on the cloak and dagger stuff? Probably.

But Angie could only think of what she would do if she were in Aunt Margery's position. Two nosy women trying to fool each other for their own good.

She probably couldn't be *too* careful.

#

On the way to the bookstore, she pulled over in a parking lot and gently investigated the clothes. The dress didn't have a tag to it; the seams were a little crooked here and there, as if it had been hand-sewn. The fabric was lighter and stuck to itself. Where the heat had been the strongest, holes had melted in it with charred black edges. Overall it was brown, orange, and rusty red color, with a few teal spots swirled in.

As she examined the dress, she noticed about half the teal spots were covered with a big stain. She scratched at it with one fingernail. Whatever it was, it had charred up from the fire and was now flaking off. Even after it was gone, it left behind a dark smudge.

So...her aunt had gone out to the beach to burn a dress. Why? Were they the clothes that she had dated Raymond Quinn in, all those years ago?

No. Angie had seen pictures of her great-aunt back in the Seventies: she was short but much more slender, bosomy on top, and definitely not big enough through the hips to fit this dress.

The dress had to be old. Angie hadn't seen her great-aunt wear it before.

Wait.

She went back to the dress, lifted it carefully to her face, and sniffed it. It smelled like burnt wood and slightly of burnt plastic. The flaking stains smelled a little different, but she didn't recognize it.

Which meant she couldn't be sure that it wasn't blood.

Oh no. A feeling of dread, like a thousand needles pricking her skin.

There were better ways to get rid of clothes that didn't fit you anymore and that you hadn't worn for years. Like donating them to a thrift store, or cutting them up for craft projects, or even seeing if Ruth wanted them to sell them online as vintage.

Or even just throwing them in the trash.

Aunt Margery had gone out to the beach last night not just to meet up with Quinn, but to burn clothing—and not just any old clothing, but *stained* clothing. Stains that seemed like they might be blood.

She had done it in a way that should have carried the ashes out into the bay, too. Anything left behind would be just another negligent act by tourists. Nobody would bother to, say, bag up any remaining fibers and test them for bloodstains.

Angie slipped the dress back into the bag and sealed it.

Her great-aunt had been out of the house late on the night of the third. Out on the beach waiting for her pirate, she said, who Angie now knew to be Quinn.

Had the two of them killed Alexander Snuock together?

Chapter 10

IMAGINATION, SUPPOSITION, AND MEMORY

The morning was a tense one. The plastic bag with the clothing went into Angie's trunk in the spare-tire compartment, under the carpeting.

Angie worked through the morning rush, which showed no signs of slowing down after the holiday weekend. It took all she had to stay focused on the task at hand. A day off, she kept telling herself. All she needed to stop being so paranoid was a day off. That was it. But who could relax, let alone sleep, with Pastries & Page-Turners as busy as it was? And then there was the slight detail of incriminating evidence for a murder lying in her trunk.

In the back of her mind, she worried at the same scene over and over again. As she pulled espresso shots and foamed milk, she imagined Raymond Quinn and her great-aunt driving up to the Snuock mansion together. Aunt Margery rolls down her window and presses the intercom button.

"Who is it?" Snuock calls.

Quinn bellows, "It's me," and then adds a number of epithets.

Alexander Snuock gives a wicked chuckle then opens the gate. The two of them drive to the back door and are admitted to the house. Snuock chats pleasantly and says, "Would you like something to drink?"

Angie tried to remember whether she had seen any drinks in the study. She didn't think so, or at least she didn't remember seeing a cluster of three glasses, which she thought would have stood out in her memory.

And so Aunt Margery would have said, "This isn't a social visit, Alex, and you know it."

Snuock chuckles again and says, "Then let's get to business. Upstairs. In my study." They could have discussed things in the kitchen, but Snuock would have had to show off. He couldn't have helped himself: how often did you get to humiliate a lifelong enemy in your own home? Just leading him through the house would have allowed Snuock to rub Quinn's face in his wealth.

They go upstairs and Snuock sits behind his desk. If there were other chairs to sit at, Angie had never seen them during one of her book drop-off visits with Snuock previously. It wasn't a comfortable room. Every time she had been in Snuock's office, she had been forced to stand the entire time .

So Aunt Margery and Quinn stand on the other side of the desk.

"What seems to be the problem?" Snuock asks.

"You can't raise our rents like this," Quinn says.

"Oh, yes I can."

Then the two of them argue back and forth like a pair of children for a few moments. "No you can't." "Yes I can." Finally, Aunt Margery would have broken it up. "Boys!" she would have said. And then she would have quoted a book at the two of them: something sharp and humiliating. Maybe some Oscar Wilde.

Then things suddenly go downhill. The Rubicon has been crossed somehow, and now the lifelong enmity between Snuock and Quinn turns deadly.

Snuock had proof that Quinn was sleeping with his ex-wife. Given what Angie knew now, it couldn't have been anything else. Not only was Snuock raising the rents on his tenants with the intention of driving Quinn out of business, but he had also intended to cut off Phyllis's allowance, leaving both of them bitter and impoverished.

In Quinn's eyes, Snuock would have just added insult to injury. In Angie's hypothetical scenario, Quinn walks menacingly up to the desk, leans over, and grabs Snuock by the collar...Snuock has just called Phyllis something ugly.

"Take it back," Quinn says.

Snuock refuses.

Aunt Margery tries to settle things down. Neither man is having any of it.

Snuock jerks himself out of Quinn's grasp. Quinn starts to move around the desk. Snuock reaches over to the broad windowsill where he keeps his antiques for display, surrounding himself with history as well as wealth. He picks up the antique Russian revolver.

Snuock aims it at Quinn. "Not one step closer," he would have said.

"I'll kill you," Quinn swears.

They wrestle. Aunt Margery tries to pull them apart. Really, she's effectively trying to save Snuock from getting strangled. Quinn is so much bigger than Snuock that if it weren't for the gun, Snuock would have already been dead.

The gun goes off. Snuock's eyes widen and he slumps down onto the floor, coming to rest where Angie and Valerie found him. The gun falls beside him.

Quickly, Aunt Margery takes her dress and uses it to wipe the fingerprints from the gun. She and Quinn flee.

There's blood all over their clothing.

She hides it for several days...then takes it out to the beach and burns it. She's furious at Quinn, both for the affair and for...the accident.

They argue. Quinn storms off the beach. A few minutes later, the normally rock-solid Aunt Margery kicks some sand over the fire and follows. If things hadn't gone so badly, she might have remembered to check that the clothing had been completely burned.

Over and over the scene played in Angie's mind. It was possible. It was even plausible.

She remembered Aunt Margery cautioning her that she should figure out what she wanted to happen with regard to Walter's arrest. Now her words took on an extra meaning.

What did Angie want to come of this?

The morning stretched on, seeming to get stranger and stranger as it went. Both Mickey and Jo came in several times to check up on the pastries—and Angie it seemed. Jo brought the news that Walter had been officially charged with the murder of his father, murder in the second degree. Angie couldn't take it in, after feeling so hopeful that she could give him an alibi for the third, this was just too much. Instead of acknowledging what Jo told her, she tried to explain her idea about the cupcakes, while Jo watched her cautiously.

She knew she wasn't making any sense. She'd been drinking too much coffee that morning, so much coffee that she had reached a point where she felt that she was moving with complete clarity and calm, but knew that she shouldn't be trusted with heavy machinery. Captain Parfait butted her in the ankle several times throughout the morning. He even brought her a gray yarn "mouse" that had been liberated from her bookmarks, a special fuzzy that had been hidden away for months, apparently.

Nine o'clock passed, then ten. Eleven o'clock approached.

Soon, Aunt Margery would arrive at the bookstore.

#

When the back door opened at eleven fifteen, Angie's arms popped up with gooseflesh.

The bookstore was relatively empty, with only two customers wandering the shelves, and neither of them likely to finish or need a cup of coffee any time soon.

In the last few moments, Angie had come to a decision: she would confront her great-aunt. She was going to drive herself mad otherwise.

On the one hand, Aunt Margery might confess. On the other, she might have a perfectly reasonable explanation.

Her stomach wrapped up in knots, Angie walked into the back room and said, "I need to ask you about something."

Aunt Margery straightened up from where she was going through the boxes of books that had arrived in the mail. "Yes?"

Was her voice especially sharp that morning, or was Angie just imagining it?

"Why did you try to burn that clothing last night?"

Aunt Margery, her back still turned, froze.

"I finally got a good look at the dress this morning, and it was stained with blood. I heard some of what you and Quinn said to each other last night. I know that he was sleeping with Phyllis."

"Is that what you think?" Aunt Margery said.

"That's what I heard. I think the two of you," she swallowed, "were involved in a terrible accident."

"An accident."

"An accident," Angie said firmly. "Otherwise, it would have happened differently."

Aunt Margery finally turned around. Her face was pinched in places, and a rash of red and white blotches covered her cheeks. "Is that what you think?" she repeated.

"Given what I know now, yes. Unless there is something else you want to tell me."

Aunt-Margery lifted her hands to her face. Angie couldn't tell whether her great-aunt wanted to scream or cry. She had never seen her look so desperate.

"And what am I supposed to tell you?" said Aunt Margery. "Huh? Have you even considered what kind of position it would put you in if you really knew who murdered Snuock?"

Angie's palms went flush and damp. She hadn't thought that far ahead. She wanted to know the truth. Isn't the truth what mattered? And was this her aunt admitting that she and Raymond had murdered Snuock? She suddenly felt claustrophobic in the small back room.

Aunt Margery continued, "I can see you haven't considered the consequences. You never have." There was that parental tone—the one Angie's own parents never used—the tough love.

"I didn't go to eavesdrop on your conversation last night. I just happened upon it, and I can't do anything about what I know now."

"I understand." Aunt Margery tilted her head and looked pensively at Angie. "You can't do anything about what you don't know either. So let's not talk anymore about it."

And then she walked toward the back door, opened it, and went out.

#

Angie's calls to Aunt Margery went straight to voicemail. She packaged up the clothing in a cushioned mailer envelope, sealed it, and put a note on the front: *Do not send, still looking for address.* She puttered, but everything she touched seemed to go badly. She even dropped a first edition hardcover (thankfully not signed) and bent some of the pages. At two o'clock, she finally gave it up and closed early.

Aunt Margery wasn't at home. Her car was gone, and Angie didn't see any signs that she'd been back. The door of her room wasn't locked. Angie went inside and stood there, afraid to touch anything. Curiosity was almost killing her, but she didn't dare upset Aunt Margery any further.

After pacing the kitchen for a few minutes, then lying down on top of her covers and trying to sleep, Angie got back in the car and drove back to the parking lot behind the bookstore. Fortunately, she didn't see Jo at the back door—she didn't know if she'd be able to keep it together if she saw her best friend. And the last thing she wanted was for Jo to go marching off to confront Aunt Margery, demanding "the truth." Instead, Angie walked to the back door of Ruth's shop. She hesitated with her hand on the knob, then turned it and went in.

Next to the door was the wall full of old photographs. Angie looked it over, this time being more thorough, gently lifting photos to get at those in the lower layers.

One of the photographs fell down anyway and fluttered to the floor.

A hand reached down and picked it up. Ruth was standing beside her.

A glance at her face told Angie that she knew what had happened between Angie and her great-aunt.

"I'm looking for something," Angie said.

"Oh, sweetie," Ruth said. "I'm...this is just impossible, you know that?"

Angie ignored her for the moment. She'd found it: the photograph of Quinn next to Dory, in front of a boat. She hadn't known, when she had seen it the other day, who the tall, handsome man had been, but now it was obvious: her great-aunt's handsome pirate...who had been dating her best friend at the time.

"A love triangle," she said. "Where did Alexander Snuock come into all of this?"

A glance at Ruth told her that she wasn't going to find out from her: her lips were pressed together, sealed shut.

"Did Aunt Margery and Raymond Quinn kill him?" Angie asked.

The lips went a little bit thinner.

Angie started to lose her temper. *None* of this was fair. "Loyalty is a waste of time if it means that the people who love you the most can't help you."

Ruth still didn't answer. Angie left by the back door, got in the car, and started driving. She was going to stop at a cove, get out, and watch the waves roll in. Instead, she found herself on the ferry headed over to Hyannis. From there she drove to Boston, checked to see whether there were any theater tickets she wanted. She splurged on a ticket for the new staging of *The Phantom of the Opera*—a single seat in the Mezzanine—and spent the evening allowing herself to be carried away by the emotion and drama of the show. If the people around her thought that she was a slightly over-emotional fan of musicals, so much the better.

By the time it was over, she was satisfied to realize that she had missed the last ferry. She checked her phone: Jo had called and left a message. But not Aunt Margery.

Angie texted Jo back: *Rough day...tell you later. Fled to Boston for Phantom, staying the nite.*

Jo replied: *Without meee!!!???!!!*

Sorry. Too upset. Didn't want to drag you down. Or spend the night crying.

Is it Walter?

Not directly. Tell you later. Still too upset. Angie felt tears welling up.

Tell me.

Angie could almost hear Josephine sighing through the phone.

Angie started to type in a shorter version of the story, then stopped and deleted what she had written. If Aunt Margery was guilty, or in some way involved with what was going on, she didn't want to leave any evidence that she had known or suspected anything about it on her phone.

In her heart, she knew that if Aunt Margery were guilty she would back her up. To the hilt. Angie wanted to be the kind of dry-eyed, analytical genius who could sort the innocent from the guilty based on the color of mud on the bottom of a suspect's shoes, then turn around and dispassionately send the guilty to the cops, but she wasn't. Family counted too much with her.

Then again, even Sherlock Holmes had let some of his quarry escape. Or they had fooled him, like Irene Adler.

Still in her car in the theater district parking lot, Angie wiped her eyes, then texted to Jo:

I'm sorry...this isn't the kind of thing you can do over the phone. When I get back.

Tomorrow?

She would have to open the bookstore in the morning. The earliest ferry was—she looked it up—6:15, which meant that she wouldn't get in until 7:15, and wouldn't be able to open until 7:30 or 7:45 at the earliest.

She was being totally irresponsible. A child. And if Aunt Margery was in trouble, she wouldn't even hear anything about it until the morning.

She breathed in, held it for a count of ten, and exhaled.

I'm going to get a motel room for the night...back ASAP in the morning. I won't be able to open until 7:30 or 7:45.

OK. We'll talk when Aunt Margery takes over.

I'm not sure if she's talking to me or if she'll even be in tomorrow. Angie shook her head at the phone.

Whoa.

Jo would probably go running straight to her mother to find out what was going on. Angie had to warn her without seeming to warn her. She chewed on her lip. She couldn't think of anything to say that couldn't possibly be used against one of them later, in case of a trial.

I think everyone's feeling a bit touchy at the moment, she finally texted back. *I'd be careful about asking questions.*

So don't be my normal bull in a china shop self?!? Hahahaha...

The answer rang false. Angie hoped that meant Jo had realized that their phones could be used against them and was being discreet. A second later, Jo texted:

OK, OK, won't confront the Three Witches to find out the gossip. Sheldon maybe.

Angie thumped her hand against her head. If only she had thought of that before she had spoken to Aunt Margery. Sheldon had been around the island forever, and probably knew more of the old dirt than anyone other than Aunt Margery and her clique. Jo texted again:

Don't worry, got you covered. Have a good night. Will text if emergency, otherwise will wait until a.m.

Thanks.

Angie found a reasonably cheap hotel nearby and booked a room with her credit card. She hadn't eaten. She grabbed a late meal at a dumpling house, of ginseng chicken soup, steamed pork buns, and fried bitter melon. As a girl, she'd never been an adventurous eater. But as she ate she realized that this whole trip to Boston had been almost exactly like one that she'd taken with Aunt Margery when she was twelve.

The theater—*Les Misérables* back then—for a matinée showing, and then to an Asian restaurant for an early supper before heading back across on the ferry before nightfall. The restaurant she was in now was too new to be the same one, but it was in the same area. Maybe even the same location. Her memories were too fuzzy to be sure.

If Aunt Margery wasn't involved, then why had she burned the clothing?

The only thing that Angie didn't understand was why, if she and Quinn had gone to confront Snuock, she'd worn the old paisley dress in the first place.

Or why he'd let them in...

Chapter 11

THE LITTLE GREY LADY OF THE SEA

Jo had already opened up the bookstore by the time Angie arrived back on the island. She walked in the back door to find the early rush already tended to and contentedly slurping their drinks in the café area, reading newspapers. The only difference was that Jo had left out the wrong sorts of books—mind-blowing New Wave sci-fi, mostly, stuff that *she* liked to read and recommend. Several Harlan Ellisons were prominently displayed.

The problem was that you could lead customers to a good book, but you couldn't make them read. Angie had long ago made up her mind that, given the choice between dictating the tastes of the island and giving them what they wanted to read (even if she had to hold her nose as she filled out the order form), she would choose the latter. Although if someone asked for a recommendation, she might tilt the scales a little toward books of which she was especially fond.

It didn't matter, though. Angie gave her friend a hug. Jo turned it into something almost unbearably tight.

"I can't breathe!" Angie gasped.

"I'm just happy to see you," Jo beamed. "You okay?"

"I think I'll be okay."

"I talked to Sheldon. He was a little cryptic, but I think your aunt's just looking out for you."

"I know. I can't talk about this now."

"Gotcha." Jo squeezed Angie's shoulders. "Why don't we go to Sheldon's for lunch. You're going to need a break and I know you're mind won't rest until you've cross-examined all sources.

Angie smiled and nodded.

She took over on the espresso drinks, finishing up the last of the line, while Jo fled back to the bakery. Angie wouldn't have been surprised if she'd been up all night.

Angie had to do her best to keep the regular hours at the store. If Aunt Margery didn't show up, she'd close for the lunch hour and then be back at it until closing time. She couldn't afford to lose business now, after all the good work that she'd done over the fourth, passing out fliers, shaking hands, and kissing babies. She had to let the store find its new momentum.

As usual, she got caught up with the daily business of the store, and was going through an ordering catalogue when the front door slammed shut.

She looked up. Phyllis Snuock had walked into her store.

For the first time ever.

She had a mad look in her eye. The same purse dangled from her arm, still bloated with yarn. Captain Parfait lifted his head and watched her as she crossed the room.

She headed in a beeline for Angie's counter.

"Hello, Phyllis," Angie said. "How can I help you? Are you looking for knitting books?"

There was more purpose behind Phyllis's stride and sour expression than the search for a knitting book could ever arouse, but Angie couldn't think of anything else to say.

"No," Phyllis snapped. "I would like a café au lait and a pastry."

It almost sounded like she was saying, *don't lie to me...confess!* Her tone was so direct and angry that Angie had to wonder if there was some kind of horrible rumor going around about her and Walter, and the woman had come to confront her about stealing her son or something.

Angie showed her the selections. Phyllis picked a puff pastry with lemon curd and berries. Angie made the café au lait, and happily rang up her charge card. Phyllis signed on the iPad screen with a finger that jabbed like a claw.

Angie offered her a receipt—"No!"—and carried the small plate and large cup over to Phyllis's chosen armchair. It was paired with a second chair across a diminutive table.

"Sit," Phyllis ordered.

There was no one in line, and no one looking around as if they needed assistance. Drat.

Angie sat gingerly in the other chair.

Phyllis pointed a finger at her. "You know my son."

"Yes."

"And you must think well of him."

"I do."

"I won't say that it's love. What is love? It is something that cannot be defined. You can only hope that your heart isn't lying to you when love strikes. You do not have the look of love. It's a stupid look."

Angie blinked.

Phyllis chuckled, almost evilly. Several of the men reading newspapers nearby shifted their weight slightly, leaning away from her as they read. Their papers rustled.

"Now, knitting. You know where you are with yarn. Yarn is the adversary. It's always trying to drop stitches and make you lose count. Come unraveled. Or roll across the floor and tangle itself in knots. And yet you can do nothing about it. To me, that is how love should be seen: a big fat mess. And yet no one does see it that way, instead they all get carried away."

Coming from a woman whose ex-husband had both paid for her to live and had threatened to cut off those payments when she rebelled, Angie could understand her point of view. Not that she agreed with it.

"But that's not what I came here to talk about. What I came here to say was: my son is innocent. He had nothing to do with the death of his father."

The men rustled their papers again as they leaned closer. Phyllis leaned toward Angie, lowering her voice.

"And I'll tell you a secret. *I didn't either!*" She leaned back, her eyes as big and round as donuts, as if she had just given Angie the key to the mystery.

Angie suppressed her first reaction, which was to laugh. "What were you doing on the night of the third, Phyllis?"

She snorted. "That's not what you want to know, is it? I was at home, with no alibi whatsoever. I'm a lonely old woman. What you want to know is...*where was Walter!*"

"That's true." Angie said. " Although, I was under the impression that he went home after he left me."

"Because you were on a date!" A finger pointed in Angie's direction again, then the hand swooped down to pick up the latte and slurp noisily from it. "*Why* didn't you just say that he was with you all night?"

"Because...he wasn't. And because—"

"But you could have said it! A normal person would have said that. A normal person would have provided an alibi without thinking twice. A normal person would have shown loyalty." Her words almost ended in a growl and her eyes seemed to burn with passion. If she hadn't been creeping Angie out, it would have been fascinating.

"If you'll let me finish," said Angie.

"Go ahead," Phyllis snarled.

"No one asked me where I was on the third."

"Humph." Phyllis stuck her pointy nose in the air.

"And even if, say, Detective Bailey had asked, I would have told the truth. And I did tell him the truth about the fourth. He never asked about the third. I don't like to lie," Angie said.

"Nobody does! But that's what you do. I want you to remember that when Walter is released from prison. You haven't got it in you to love him, not the way he should be loved."

Angie felt heat coming up into her face. She shoved her hands alongside her legs and clutched them into fists where Phyllis couldn't see them. Was that what the woman had come to the bookstore to do? To castigate her for *not lying for her son*? The nerve!

"Maybe not," Angie said. She wasn't going to argue. This woman was crazy. Poor Walter.

"Don't toy with *me*," Phyllis said. "I need you to find a book for me."

Angie gave a little shudder. Could the woman be any more strange and random? "A knitting book?" she asked, her voice coming out sharper than she intended.

"Ahhh...now we see her true colors," Phyllis said. "A knitting book. She wants to know if I want a knitting book. In fact, I do not want a knitting book." She squinted. "Or...it depends. What do you have?"

Angie took a breath. "We can look at them in a moment, Phyllis. What other book did you want?"

"A book on local history. *The Little Grey Lady of the Sea: The Mysteries of Nantucket Island*, by David Dane."

Angie knew the book and even had a copy or two in the bookstore. She hadn't read it, but she knew enough about it to know that it didn't have the most factual information available. It was a sensational view of Nantucket history, from the earliest history, through the whaling days, and up to the 1980s. It had been sold by a local tour company in the 1980s and early 1990s as part of their promotional material —"You've taken the ghost walk! Buy the book!" That kind of thing. It was the sort of fluff that Alexander Snuock would have sneered at, yet almost a collector's item.

"I may have a copy of that."

"Good. Go get it," Phyllis said.

Angie could be of service if it would get Phyllis out of the store. She unclenched her fists, stood up, and walked between the cluster of newspaper-reading men toward the shelves as calmly as possible. She could feel Phyllis staring at her.

She picked up one of the two copies and returned with it. "Here it is."

Phyllis took the copy from her and riffled through the pages, stopping near the back of the book. She flipped through a few pages and stopped at a page with a black and white photograph on it. Angie tried to catch a glimpse of the page number, but Phyllis clapped the book shut.

"It's *there*," she said. "I'll take it."

"Okay," Angie said, perplexed. "And the knitting book?"

She expected the woman to storm out of the store without paying for the book; instead, her eyes widened slightly and she smiled with sardonic pleasure. She stood up, positively towering over Angie.

"Let's see what you have," she said.

"If you don't mind," Angie said, now struggling to keep the bemusement out of her voice more than anything else, "I'm not a knitter, and I could use any good advice you have on how to shore up what I have. Tourists often look for this sort of thing, and I have no idea what to order from the catalog..."

"You can order knitting books?"

"Oh, yes."

Phyllis picked out one of the books, on Irish cable knitting, then spent another fifteen minutes leaning over the counter and looking at book catalogues. Angie ordered a slim collection of eight different books, with five copies of one book, two copies of two others, and one each of the rest, under advisement. The first book would be for tourists who knew how to knit a plain scarf, if that; the next two were good intermediate books with easy projects that let the knitters learn new stitch patterns, and the other three were "excellent ruminations on the nature of pattern design and the philosophy of crafting." Whatever that meant.

When the woman finally stepped out of the front door and let it fall gently closed behind her, Angie felt like she'd sidestepped a land mine. And the newspaper-reading gents in the café area seemed to exhale a collective sigh as well.

On her way out the door, Phyllis had tapped the cover of *The Little Grey Lady of the Sea* and said, "This book contains nothing but the truth. If anyone were looking for the truth, they could do worse than to search its well-researched pages." And had given Angie a significant look.

Angie tidied up the café area, asked her gentlemen if they had everything they needed—really just assuring them that it was over now and they could relax—and checked the rest of her customers. All was well, other than the fact that she needed to brew another pot of coffee, which she'd missed earlier.

She went back to the ordering catalogue and tried to work out the rest of her next order, but her heart wasn't in it. This last distraction from Phyllis had been one too many. She checked the clock on the register—it wasn't even ten a.m. yet.

This day was going to drag.

She went into the back room, booted up the computer, and loaded the accounting program. If there was one thing she had learned about running a small business, it was that there was always something that needed to be done with the receipts...

She couldn't focus. "Fine," she told herself, got up, and plucked the other copy of *The Little Grey Lady of the Sea* off the local history shelf. She poured herself a cup of hot coffee, added a little cream then started paging through it.

The book was a collection of scandal, rumor, gossip, and outright lies, the kind where every Native American burial ground is haunted, a dozen young women were murdered by sailors, the Quakers were all British loyalists during the Revolutionary War, the Great Nantucket Fire of 1846 was set by a business rival and not caused by a defective stovepipe, and so on. Her great-grandfather, Captain John F. Prouty, was mentioned as a possible cannibal. Angie rolled her eyes.

Parts of the more recent sections of the book were about Alexander Snuock. Angie found herself settling in for some juicy gossip, and had to remind herself that she couldn't believe *anything* the book said. The authors didn't care about facts, although they did care about getting sued for libel; the worst of the information was presented as speculation and gossip. In Angie's opinion, they had walked a very thin line, especially where Snuock was concerned.

The pages accused Walter's father of having driven several of his competitors out of business by controlling property tax assessments in Nantucket, establishing a monopoly on the ferry lines (Angie had had no idea that he owned them in the first place), and other under-handed tricks.

Alexander Snuock might not be a murderer or cannibal on the level of Captain John F. Prouty, the authors noted, but if the rumors were correct, then he might be considered as part of the long tradition of pirates on Nantucket.

Ugh.

What had Phyllis even been trying to tell her? What was "the truth" that Angie was supposed to discover inside it.

And who was this David Dane? Angie had never heard of him.

She longed to call up her great-aunt and ask—of course Aunt Margery would have been on the island when the book was published and had to know all about it—but she couldn't. Not when there wasn't a single returned call or text on Angie's phone.

And not while Aunt Margery refused to talk about whether she had been involved in a murder.

#

Jo showed up for lunch at one o'clock; a few customers were still in the store. Angie handed her *The Little Grey Lady of the Sea* and told her about the confrontation with Phyllis.

"Honestly, it was one of the strangest things that I've ever had happen to me," Angie said.

Jo frowned. "Imagine being Walter and growing up with that. I have to wonder why someone like Alexander Snuock would have married her in the first place, let alone paid her upkeep and maintenance after they divorced and Walter was on his own. It had to be the sex."

"Josephine!"

"Well? It's the most logical reason."

Angie stared off into the bookracks, thinking about Snuock and the books he liked. "It makes sense to me," she said. "Snuock was a collector."

"He collected her?"

"No...or maybe? Kind of? He could have had any woman he wanted, well, any woman who could be swayed by a lot of money. And there are plenty of them. He could have picked a blonde bombshell. But that would have been too straightforward and easy. See, he liked to read about, oh, eccentric people. Like the inventor Tesla; he went through a Tesla phase a few years ago. And the Russians, who spent whole centuries impaling their enemies and enslaving peasants."

Jo laughed. "He would have done that, too, if he could have gotten away with it."

"I don't know. He was more about the psychological torture. I see him more in the CIA during the Cold War."

"Was he in the CIA during the Cold War?"

"Sure, why not," Angie said. "I'm surprised that the author of *The*

Little Grey Lady of the Sea didn't include it. Did you see what he said about my great-grandfather?"

"No!"

"Anyway, he probably honed in on Phyllis because he sensed an opportunity to exploit and torture." She thought about it some more, and a wry smile crossed her lips. "Or maybe it's like you said: mind blowing sex!"

"Miss Agatha Prouty, you didn't!" Jo mocked, slapping her hand against a shocked expression on her face.

The last of the customers checked out; Angie closed up the shop and the two of them drove over to Sheldon's for lunch.

The host showed them to a table in a back corner where they could have a private discussion, their backs to the wall and a clear "moat" of empty tables surrounding them. Most of the customers had been moved to the patio outside. It was a beautiful day.

"So," Jo said.

"So," Angie replied. It was time for the hard part of the conversation. She told Jo about finding Aunt Margery on the children's beach with Quinn, their discussion, and Angie's flight to the lighthouse when it seemed like Quinn was walking straight toward her...then her return to the children's beach, the idea about the cupcakes, and finding the dress inside the fire.

"That's a good idea about the cupcakes," Jo said. "I'll talk to Mickey about it."

"Thank you," Angie said. "I tried to tell you about it earlier—"

"But you weren't making sense. At all." Jo leaned back. "And finding the dress in the fire...not too shabby Detective Prouty." Jo winked.

Angie continued her story. "...and then I wrapped the dress up in the blanket and took it home." She told her about the freezer bag, then transferring the dress to the bubble-wrap mailer at the bookstore and leaving it without an address.

"Very nice," said Jo. "If I ever need someone to hide evidence for me, you're my first choice."

"Thanks."

They paused for a moment while the waiter came over and told them the day's specials. They already knew what they wanted and so ordered right away.

When he left, Jo leaned across the table and whispered. "And what did you say to Aunt Margery that set her off so badly?"

Angie whispered back, "I asked her why she'd tried to burn the clothing in the bonfire, and told her that I'd seen that the dress was stained with blood. And that I'd heard her and Quinn and knew that Quinn was sleeping with Phyllis."

Jo sank back into her chair. "If I didn't know you, I'd say that you have no idea how to play poker. You don't just show all your cards like that."

"You do," Angie insisted, "if you're trying to find out whether your great-aunt needs help getting off a murder or accessory to murder rap. She's not my enemy. She's supposed to be my ally. This was supposed to be more like bridge than poker."

"Okay, I can see that. What you did makes more sense. I just normally think in terms of not telling everyone everything."

Angie coughed. "Like picking up strangers on the fourth of July..."

"Ha, ha." Jo smirked. "Back to business: you haven't heard from Aunt Margery since your conversation?"

"Nope."

"Hmm. She has to know that you wouldn't just run straight to the cops to turn her in. Besides she knows people on the police force and that you haven't said anything. Otherwise, she'd be in the can with Walter Snuock."

Angie pictured Walter in his orange scrubs, like a criminal in a TV crime drama, and cringed. Then she imagined her great-aunt in the same get-up. Not a good look, not an option. "Then why hasn't she called me back?"

"Indeed, why hasn't she called you back? I have no idea. Unless she really was involved somehow, and wants to make sure that you're not implicated if she gets caught."

Angie dug her nails into her palms. "She kind of said as much."

Jo didn't answer. A moment later their food arrived. The subtle smell of grilled fish wafted from their plates. Wind chimes on the patio sounded in the breeze.

They finished their meal more or less in silence, keeping mainly to small talk. Angie was so preoccupied she barely noticed the taste of her food. "I should check on Walter," she said, "but I think that by the time I close up the shop for the day, visiting hours will be over."

"Then don't open the shop up again. Just close it."

"During the middle of summer?" She felt scandalized.

"Don't tell me that you're that broke," Jo said.

"No, but..."

"But you want to sit on your hoard of emergency money forever, just in case an emergency happens. *Hello*. What constitutes an emergency? Your great-aunt might be involved in a murder, an old friend is in jail for it, even when he's innocent, and you're planning to work twelve-hour days while trying to solve the case so that you can prove

Walter's innocence *and* protect your great-aunt in the process. You see my point, don't you?"

Angie had to concede. "Yes, I do. Maybe I'll close the shop." She gazed out toward the patio; some clouds had descended on the shore and she couldn't distinguish between them and the ocean. "Maybe there's a perfectly innocent explanation for Aunt Margery's actions."

Jo rolled her eyes. "There isn't, Angie. There is *no* innocent explanation for her actions. None. You *do not* burn bloody clothing while arguing with a guy that you had an affair with decades ago and who had a nearly life-long feud with the murder victim. You just don't. It might not be murder, but it's not innocent."

As if on cue, Sheldon appeared on the far side of the dining room, looked at the two of them, and began to walk over. If he stopped to talk to a few of the other customers and make sure they had no complaints, he still seemed in Angie's mind to be pursuing them as directly as a shark.

"What did the two of you talk about?" Angie asked Jo.

"I think he's here to talk about that himself."

Sheldon approached the table. The broad grin that he had had on his face as he was speaking to his other customers had vanished once he was out of their sight. His hands were stuffed in the pockets of his pants and he was jingling his keys nervously.

Their table was a four-top; he pulled out a chair and sat on Angie's other side.

"So," he said.

Angie resisted the urge to say something smart. "I've told Josephine everything I know," she said.

"And now it's my turn," Sheldon said.

"Okay," said Angie.

"What I know is that your great-aunt would never wish to see you hurt," he said. " Look, they don't tell me everything. I'm just little old Sheldon, the kid who grew up two years younger than they were, and who never quite fit in with their circle. I liked to cook, you see. I didn't read all the books. The five of them, they were obsessed."

"The five of them?"

"Oh, yes," Sheldon said. "Didn't you know? It started out when they were all very young, in Kindergarten. They used to all be friends. They *were* friends for a long time, too, no matter what they say now: Your Aunt Margery, Josephine's mother Dory, their best friend Ruth, Raymond Quinn, and Alexander Snuock. None of the rest of us could break into that circle—even the ones who were in the same grade, like Phyllis. Oh, yeah, she's an islander, too, and the one who eventually caught Alexander Snuock, as you know."

"Eventually?" Angie said.

Sheldon tapped the side of his nose. "All of them denied it, but we all knew there was some kind of hanky-panky going on. Who was with whom at any given moment, nobody knew. But you couldn't miss that there was drama going on. And then suddenly Raymond Quinn and Dory Jerritt got engaged. You couldn't miss *that*."

"Engaged?" Angie asked. A glance at Jo earned her a puzzled shrug. She'd have to find out the details later. "I saw a picture on Ruth's back wall of Quinn and Dory together in front of his boat."

"Sure," Sheldon said. "I've seen it, too. But not six weeks later the engagement was over, friendships shattered forever, and Alexander Snuock was enemy number one."

"The way they tell it, it sounds like they were enemies long before that."

"They," Sheldon said, "can tell the story however they want. But if you were to look at the old high school yearbook photos, it would tell a different story. Their junior year they were all in Miss Mark's literary club and in the same photo. Have Ruth show you *that* one. They're all standing around hugging each other with stupid grins on their faces."

Sheldon probably had a bit of a chip on his shoulder for being left out—but at least his childhood jealousies had worked out in the end. He was the one who was happily married, to his gorgeous, tall, and funny French wife. They had been together for almost forty years.

The rest of them? Not so much with the marital bliss.

Sheldon gave her a few seconds, then added: "So you see what I'm saying?"

Angie shook her head. It was hitting her too hard that her Aunt Margery had been withholding so much, and what that might mean for a murder investigation.

"If Alexander Snuock had to have opened the gate for his murderer to someone who was both close enough to him to get him to open the gate, and yet might have a personal motive to kill him, it was one of *them* all right."

The stunned look on Angie's face must have satisfied him. He leaned back and glanced over the table. "Don't worry about paying for this. I've got your tab."

"Thank you," Angie said, almost too quietly for her to hear her own voice.

Then Sheldon spotted the book, *The Little Grey Lady of the Sea.* "I see you've found her book," he said. "That old thing. We used to keep a rack of them for the tourists."

"Her book?" Angie asked. "I thought it was written by a David Dane."

"A David Dane who knows this much local gossip? Please," Sheldon said. "The only people who know this much about the town—and I'm not saying that it's all true—is *that* circle of five. They spent a lot of time researching every horrible thing that ever might have happened in the town's history. Of course by the time it was published, Snuock had been out of the group for a long time, so he got splattered with some of the mud. But the original research? They all did it together in high school, during Miss Mark's class. They were going to write ghost stories set on the island, a whole book of them, all five of them taking turns."

"So who did write the book?" Angie asked.

"Why, your Aunt Margery," Sheldon said. "Cover to cover. With Dory and Ruth's help as editors, probably. But your great-aunt was always the one with the best turn of phrase in the group."

"She says that my great-grandfather was a cannibal!"

Sheldon said, "You might try asking her sometime where she came up with that idea...one of his journals, I think. That is, when all of this has blown over and you are speaking again."

Chapter 12

LIES AND MISDIRECTION

She went back to the bookstore and opened up again, feeling disoriented. Too many of her personal anchors had been cut; she was adrift on a sea that stretched backward for decades. The bookstore stayed quiet, with only a few customers drifting in off the sidewalk. The day was fresh and sunny, yet not that hot, and everyone had gone down to the beach. She couldn't blame them.

From what Sheldon had said, and what Angie had found under the bonfire, and what she had heard between her great-aunt and Quinn, she couldn't help but come to the conclusion that Raymond Quinn and her great-aunt had shot Alexander Snuock, just as she had imagined it. Now it was time to start sorting out how to shift the blame away from her great-aunt.

If it had been an accident, maybe the best solution was for her to come clean to the police, get charged with manslaughter and go to prison.

Aunt Margery in prison.

Angie shook her head. If that had been what Aunt Margery had wanted—if she had come to Angie saying that she wanted to confess —then Angie would have gone along with it. As it was, it was clear that Aunt Margery did *not* want to confess, and she wouldn't be turning herself over to the police.

Which meant that Angie would have to back her up on that, somehow.

If Aunt Margery couldn't be guilty, then who could?

Raymond Quinn could be guilty—except that Aunt Margery hadn't stepped forward to point the finger at him, either. The two of them might not still be seeing each other, but from their conversation on the beach, Angie could only think that their friendship had endured and Aunt Margery felt loyal to him.

Angie wasn't going to let them leave the finger pointed at Walter. That was right out. She wasn't having it: Walter was part of *her* set, and Angie had every right to defend him, even if she hadn't seen him for almost twenty years.

Who did that leave?

The finger had to be pointed at someone, but who was left? Dory and Ruth were out of the question. If Angie attempted to point a finger at them, and she wouldn't, her Aunt Margery would surely never talk to her again. But someone had to take the fall, the police weren't going to suddenly change their minds and say that Snuock had killed himself with his own antique gun, playing Russian roulette or something.

Valerie?

Angie's stomach clenched. No, she couldn't do that to Valerie, either. Even if she could figure out a way to do it...she couldn't. Valerie had had to put up with Snuock for years. She didn't deserve to get blamed for his death.

Someone would have to be blamed. Someone would have to be pushed out of the shadows and take their spot as the murderer.

The only logical person left was her, Angie.

She sighed and rubbed her hand over her face. She had had a good night's sleep the previous night, against all her expectations, but she still felt exhausted, like she was walking through a dream.

Even if she walked up to the police station and confessed to the killing of Alexander Snuock, describing how the two of them had, she didn't know, fought over the payment for a book or something, wrestling over the gun until it had gone off, killing Snuock...

...nobody would believe her. Because she was Angie Prouty, owner of Pastries & Page-Turners, one of the "staying" Proutys that came back to the island and never left again, who never did anything wrong.

She could be a serial killer for all anyone would ever suspect. She shuddered. Not that she ever *would*. That would be terrible. But if she wanted to...she would *never* get caught.

She struck the sinister thought from her mind. This whole murder case was taking a toll on her.

~

She closed up an hour early. She wanted to talk to Walter again, but wasn't ready. There were too many things that he needed to know and that she needed to say, but couldn't, not at the police station, in front of witnesses.

And there were other things she needed to do before then, anyway.

First: a visit to Ruth's shop.

Ruth always closed at nine; therefore, Angie closed at eight and slipped out her back door by eight-thirty. She let herself in Ruth's back door and found her at the front counter, putting price tags on genuine Hawaiian shirts—which were more expensive than Angie would have guessed, by a factor of five to ten. Angie would have understood if they were first editions, but shirts? She just had to take Ruth's pricing ability on faith.

"Hello, dear," Ruth said. She wore her reading glasses on the tip of her nose and her arms tinkled with bangles. "Did you get it all worked out?"

"Hasn't Aunt Margery talked to you?" Angie asked.

"I finally stopped checking the phone," Ruth said in a distracted tone. "There was just too much to keep up with."

"No, we haven't worked everything out."

"Have you come over to try to send a message to Margery via the side channels, then?"

"It had occurred to me," Angie admitted. "But I didn't want to pressure you."

"Ha. Tell that to your great-aunt."

Angie stopped to think through what she wanted to say, and how she wanted to say it. "Ruth, I saw Aunt Margery and Raymond Quinn on the beach the other night. I know that they were together a long time ago, and I know that she doesn't want me to know that."

"Mm-hmm," Ruth said. "Well, I'm sorry you had to find that out."

"What? That she was seeing Quinn?"

"No, that your great-aunt is the kind of person who's so paranoid about what other people think about her that she keeps secrets even if they mean that she spends the next forty years nursing a broken heart."

"Over Quinn?"

Ruth shook her head, still filling out tags. "For such a singularly unlovable man, he was much pursued at the time. But then at the age of seventeen, he was handsome and owned his own boat already. We all thought he was destined for greatness, in a literary sense at least. Of all of us, he was the one mostly likely to write the Great American Novel, a northeastern *Old Man and the Sea*, if you will. But he wasn't the one who was published."

"That was Aunt Margery with *The Little Grey Lady of the Sea,* wasn't it?"

Ruth looked up from her pricing. "My, my. We *have* been doing our research, haven't we?"

"We have," Angie said.

"Did you see the thing about your great-grandfather?"

"Yes, but that's not the point."

"What is the point?"

"I want Aunt Margery to trust me and tell me what's going on. She should know that I'll never do anything to hurt her, or to let anyone else hurt her."

"The police, for example?" Ruth asked.

Angie didn't answer.

Ruth said, "I'll tell her. But you, my dear, should also keep in mind that Aunt Margery not telling you what you think she should tell you might not be a trust issue. She doesn't want you hurt either." She lifted the newly priced shirts off the counter. "Now, if you'll excuse me, I have a few things to finish up before I can close for the evening, and I'd like to get to them."

Ruth's words and tone struck Angie hard, letting Angie know she was being foolish and was in over her head. No matter, the drive in Angie to figure out what was really going on just wouldn't quiet. She said, "The picture with Dory Jerritt and Raymond Quinn in front of the boat...they were engaged for a while, yes?"

"Yes."

"If I looked carefully under the other photos, would I find one of all five of you together, say, in a group photo for a literary club at school?"

"You might."

And if I looked even further, would I find out who was dating Alexander Snuock?"

Ruth's jaw clenched. "No need to go stirring things up, Agatha Mary Clarissa Christie Prouty,

"Where were you on July third?"

"What's my alibi?" Ruth asked. "I was having a late supper with Sam Elliott on a yacht out in the harbor. Thousand-dollar champagne. I'm going to be the love interest in his next movie, if you can believe that"

"Right." Angie didn't appreciate her wit. "So you weren't with Dory and my Aunt Margery?"

"Sam Elliott is mine, all mine."

Neither Ruth nor her Aunt Margery wanted to come clean. Maybe that was why Aunt Margery wasn't talking: she wasn't sure how long she could keep her story straight before spilling the beans.

"You three weird sisters were doing something that night."

Ruth locked her eyes on Angie, "And what would that be?"

"You tell me."

Ruth sighed, her shoulders rounded in slight defeat. "Angie, go home. This doesn't concern you, and you can't possibly make things better.

Only worse. I know you're one of the staying Proutys and that means that you're insufferably nosy, but trust me, now is not the time."

"Did saying that ever work with my great-aunt?" Angie asked.

"No," Ruth admitted. "But that doesn't mean I have to put up with it from you. Go home now, Agnes. And stop coming in my back door."

The next stop on Angie's tour was Dory Jerritt's house, a place that Angie had spent a lot of time in as a child and teenager: a place that she'd barely seen since she'd moved back onto the island. It was on the southwest side of the island, outside of town, closer to where Angie had grown up with her parents than Aunt Margery's small, tidy house.

It was a newer home, although it had been built in the same shake-shingled style. The rooms were bigger, the ceilings were high, and upstairs they were square, rather than angled to follow the roof. The living room had pine wall panels and a loft with a ladder leading up to it, that she and Josephine and Mickey had played in, and watched TV over the side rails. There was a stairway down to the beach off the back porch. The beach was changing on that side of the island, and a lot of the houses were for sale: living on the beach was amazing until the ocean started eating the land out from underneath you.

Dory was the kind of woman who would probably stay in the house until it collapsed around her. She was just that stubborn.

Angie pulled up in front of the house and knocked on the door. Dory's car was in the driveway. Aunt Margery's wasn't. The sun had set and the sky was turning from its long ocean twilight, to the purple just before full dark.

A knock at the door and Dory answered. It was a big house for a single woman with no grandkids or dogs. How she could stand to live on her own, Angie had no idea.

"Hello, Angie," she said.

"I'm here to talk about Aunt Margery."

A sigh, and Dory opened door. "Come in. Would you like some coffee? Rum? Coffee and rum?"

"Just the coffee."

"Cream, right?"

"Yes, please."

Dory led her to the living room, still decorated with wood paneling. The loft was still there, too, facing the big-screen television. However, the heavy, indestructible furniture that Angie remembered from her childhood had been replaced with a surprisingly delicate white rattan living room set with flowered pink-and-white cushions, brightened by a few small square red accent pillows. One wall was lined with bookshelves, and a bouquet of fresh flowers stood on the glass-topped rattan coffee table. A few botanical prints hung on the walls, delicate and exact, illustrating the leaves, flowers, and fruits, seeds, or nuts of different species; thistles, hawk's beard, jimsonweed, even a dandelion that showed both a yellow flower and one that had gone to seed.

Dory came back in with two cups of coffee on a small flowered tray.

"You've changed things," Angie said.

"Since I was a mother with a pair of rowdy twins? You bet I did." She straightened up and looked around the room. "I remember the three of you up in that loft. You were the giggler."

"I have a lot of good memories of this place."

"Well, it's sliding into the ocean now," Dory said. "Erosion will probably pull it off its supports in about twenty years or so, if a storm doesn't take it first."

"That's too bad."

Dory shrugged. "It's just a house. Hopefully by the time the house is gone, I'll be in a nursing home."

"A nursing home?"

"Nobody lives forever. Besides, can you see me living with Josephine or Mickey? Even if they'd have me, I'd kill myself within the month."

Angie laughed. Dory had always had a dark sense of humor. Angie had learned a long time ago not to take it too seriously: she was just joking.

"Your Aunt Margery is lucky to have you," Dory said.

"Even if she doesn't think so right now," Angie said.

"Family," Dory said. "Loving them sometimes drives you and them crazy. "

Angie smiled, and started to relax. Dory didn't always bother to put people at their ease, but she was taking mercy on Angie's obviously tense state.

"Don't worry," Dory said. "Things with your Aunt Margery will work themselves out. This will all be over soon, and then things will get back to normal."

Angie's eyes started to fill up with tears. She took a sip of coffee to try to cover it, but she could see that Dory had noticed from the look of pity on her face.

"Aunt Margery is messed up in this, isn't she?" Angie asked.

"I can't speak to that," Dory said, shifting uneasily in the rattan chair. "But if you're upset about Alexander, don't be. He had all that money, and what good did he do with it? Nothing. He could have built libraries and hospitals. He could at least have donated to the animal shelter. But no. He sat on that money like a dragon on his hoard, too cheap even to hire enough help to keep his place from falling apart."

"Falling apart?"

"My part of the island isn't the only one falling into the ocean," Dory said. "The bluff that Snuock Manor sits on is slowly sliding into the water, too. He had the money to shore it up, but did he? No. He just pushed the problem on down the road for Walter to handle. He didn't even set up a trust fund to help protect Walter's inheritance from taxes. Couldn't be bothered. He did get everything set up so that he could raise rents all over the island, sure. But a lot of that money's going to get lost to taxes."

"That's too bad."

"Pure idiocy, that's what it is. Stubbornness and pride, and greed."

"Dory, was Aunt Margery *here* on the night of the third?"

"Tracking down an alibi, are you?" Dory pushed her hands through her hair. She looked tired. "Honey, I'd love to be able to tell you that she was here, that the two of us were having a grand old time that evening, but I was with my daughter."

She looked Angie straight in the eye when she said it.

Angie, on the other hand, blinked. She knew Dory was lying: Jo had been with her mohawked lover. Unless Jo was lying about that, too? No, she couldn't have been. Angie knew all her tells, both in and out of card games, and knew that Jo had been telling the truth—mostly, anyway.

"Where was she, then?" Angie asked.

"Your Aunt Margery? She was helping a dear friend out of a sticky situation."

"Raymond Quinn?"

Dory shook her head. "This town still holds a few secrets. Don't think that because you've just learned that she and Quinn were together once, that he's the only friend that she's ever had."

"If she wasn't with you, and she wasn't with Quinn...with Ruth, then?"

Dory shook her head again.

"With Snuock? Was she still friends with him?"

Dory lifted her chin. "What if she was?"

"I thought she hated him? And what kind of sticky situation was she getting him out of, if he ended up dead?"

Dory said, "Think about how much Alexander loved life, Angie. The passion with which he lived, his joie de vivre, his generosity of spirit."

"But..."

"*Think* about it," Dory repeated.

It was obvious Alexander Snuock didn't *have* any joie de vivre, except where money was involved, so what was Dory suggesting? That Alexander Snuock had asked Aunt Margery to shoot him because he was too scared to take his own life?

The whole situation was becoming more and more confusing.

"Is it true," Angie said, "that Raymond Quinn and Aunt Margery were in love?"

Dory leaned back in her creaking rattan chair. "I'm not sure," she said.

"You're not sure?"

"Love is complicated," she said. "Raymond had always carried a kind of fascination for her, even if she denied it. They were always at each other's throats, like a couple out of a romance. You could see the sparks fly between them. Destiny, some would have said. And then, of course, they were both too stupid to unbend enough to be good for one another, and it all fell apart, practically before anyone else knew about it."

Dory continued, "What things look like to the world aren't always what they seem. The inner truth is different. You've been in love before, that fiancé of yours who was stealing your ideas and passing them off as his own. Do you feel like what he did with the other woman was worse, or what he did with your ideas?"

Angie kept silent and sipped at her coffee.

Dory nodded. "To the world, it would have seemed that the woman was worse. But in your heart, it was the theft from you that hurt worse, that was the real violation."

Angie had already settled this point with Walter Snuock. Was she really so transparent? But this wasn't about Angie.

"What did Alexander Snuock steal from you?" Angie asked. All five of them had been in the same literary club. All *five* of them.

Dory smiled a little and shook her head. "That was a very long time ago and not a subject I'm willing to talk about.

"And the book?"

"The book?"

"*The Little Grey Lady of the Sea.*"

Suddenly Dory seemed to soften, slouching backward in her chair. "What an incredible book that was. Full of stories that couldn't be proven or disproven. The ghost stories were supposed to be fiction, you know. But Margery couldn't get it published. So we went back through everything and changed the names back to the real ones, cleaned up a few details, took out the gore, and...voilà. A sordid little tour-guide book was born. It didn't sell too badly. I still get royalty checks."

"You get them?"

"All five of us do."

"Five of you? But there are such awful things about Alexander Snuock in the last chapter."

"He wrote them himself," Dory said. "'I can't pretend to be a real-life pirate,' he said. 'So at least I'll be the evil businessman.' Raymond teased him mercilessly for that. Back when they were still speaking to each other. Ironic, isn't it? Considering that's what he became."

"Evil?"

"Raising his rents so drastically in order to drive an old friend and rival out of business? And not caring who else suffered for it? What do you call that, just an ordinary day in the business world? That's New York thinking. Manhattan thinking. It's definitely not Nantucket thinking."

"But he didn't deserve to die for that," Angie said.

Dory closed her eyes for a moment and took a deep breath. "No, he didn't. But he was still an evil man, who was more concerned with owning things—and treating people like things he owned—than he was with living. I'm sure he found death a mercy of sorts. One flash of pain, and then it was over. The long battle that he had been waging against his destiny was over."

"You think he was destined for this?"

"Sometimes we're destined for things that aren't any good for us. Remember that, when this is over." Dory's eyes narrowed, the wrinkles around the corners deepened. "You might want to remind my daughter of that, too."

Chapter 13

MISTAKES, EXCUSES, & VICIOUS CIRCLES

On the way out of the house, Angie stopped at the photo wall in Dory's hallway. It wasn't the layered, complex, bohemian creation that covered Ruth's back wall in her shop. The photos all had matching frames, for one thing, and nothing overlapped.

She saw a few photos of the three of them—her, Jo, and Mickey—from their childhood, lots of photos of either or both of the twins, and a lot of faded old photos of Hank Jerritt, tall and gangly and with Mickey's infectious grin. He'd died in an industrial accident on the docks almost exactly a year ago. Dory had been living off the company's payments since then.

Before the accident, Dory used to work on the docks with Hank part-time. Since then, she had tried a few different things—working at a couple of tourist places in the summer, volunteering at a local nursing home, walking dogs. Now her main activity was helping at the bakery.

She had enough time and money to do whatever she wanted. Ironically, she was at just as many loose ends as Snuock had been: living on her own, isolated from everyone around her, with no real need to work or accomplish anything. The only difference was that Snuock had a hobby or two—collecting things and reading books—and Dory had a family she hadn't chased away.

"Are you going to start writing again?" Angie asked.

"Oh, I never really was the writer," Dory said. "I loved books, but not really the writing. I always enjoyed editing more."

"You could do that now."

"I could." Dory reached out and touched one of the photos of her with Hank and their kids. "I've been so caught up in getting the twins on their own two feet...and about Hank, that I forgot about myself for a while. I could travel. I've always wanted to do that. If only Margery and Ruth weren't tied down with the shops."

"I'm thinking about hiring an assistant," Angie said.

"That would be nice. Then Margery could go traveling with me."

Toward the edge of the cluster of photos was a picture of five teenagers standing with their arms around each other, grinning fiercely. Handsome young Raymond Quinn was in the center at the back, with a girl on either side—Dory and Aunt Margery. A younger, skinnier, not-quite-as-handsome-as-he-would-be-later Alexander Snuock knelt in front, supporting a dramatically posed Ruth—one arm dangling on the floor and her head thrown back in a mock faint.

"There we are," Dory said. "The infamous yearbook picture. I like to remember the good with the bad, you know, even if Margery always turns up her nose as she walks down the hall and pretends she can't see it. She doesn't like being reminded."

"Of what?"

"That she can't just pretend that it was as simple as she wanted it to be. All of us made mistakes back then. Even her."

#

It was full dark out when Angie got back into the car. The stars were shining all across the cloudless night, the constellations twinkled at her, and the Milky Way ran in a dim stripe across the sky.

She should go home, even though she was nervous about seeing Aunt Margery. They'd both survive the encounter, no doubt. Angie would have to go home for clean clothes sooner or later. Technically, she could have bought new clothes and just lived out of her car for a while, but the thought made her wince.

The deeper she got into the story of these five old friends, the more she dreaded what she might dig up about Aunt Margery and the murder. She could just forget it all, stop her sleuthing and move out, close up the shop, move back to Manhattan and go back to work for her old bosses (who would probably snap her up before someone else could).

Or she could stop being ridiculous.

She drove back into town and went to the house. Aunt Margery's car was in the drive. Angie parked in her normal spot. She hesitated at the back door and then made herself put the key in.

The house was empty. Angie shoulders dropped with relief. Whatever Aunt Margery's role in the murder, Angie would just look the other way.

It would be fine. The police would sort it all out.

That was a plan, right?

If only Aunt Margery would tell her the truth. She had the power to clear up all of the confusion, but simply refused to do it. It was maddening.

Angie took a shower and got ready for bed. A long time after she had turned off the lights, she heard someone come in through the back door: Aunt Margery's soft footsteps across the floor to her bedroom, where she opened the door and closed it behind her.

#

Angie had a troubled night's sleep. Was Aunt Margery the killer? No, she couldn't believe it. It hadn't been her hand that had held the gun. It must have been Quinn. She had just been standing where the blood had...

She tried to visualize where everyone had been standing in Snuock's study. Snuock's body lay in front of the desk. The gun lay beside him. It might not have fallen there. It might have been picked up and wiped for fingerprints first, then tossed to the carpet.

There had been blood spatters on the ivory colored carpet, that much she could remember—but not what pattern were they in. No matter how much she went over it in her mind, all she could visualize was a big splotch of blood that had covered most of the carpet under Snuock's body, and some splatters around the edge. What direction? What about other patches of blood, say, on the walls or something? If Aunt Margery's dress had been covered with blood that meant that at least some of the blood had to have gone flying.

Wait, she thought, the pictures. She'd taken pictures for this very reason. She got out of bed and picked her phone up off her dresser. Quickly she opened the photos and scrolled to the ones from that night. What a shoddy job; she definitely had to work on her crime photo skills. It was obvious she hadn't been as calm under pressure as she had imagined herself. But here was one photo of the edge of the desk and the wall to the right of it, a strange angle as if she'd taken it accidentally, and spatters of blood feathered up the wall in the direction of the door. A struggle, thought Angie, there was definitely a struggle.

Had Quinn's clothes been covered with blood, too? If they had been, he could have dumped them somewhere out at sea...

Quinn's boat, the *Woolgatherer*, had been away from the dock on the night of the third. She had seen that it was missing, but hadn't put any particular value on that, because she, like everyone else, had first assumed that Snuock had been killed on the fourth.

Could Quinn have docked the *Woolgatherer* in Polpis Harbor somewhere near Snuock's house? The house did overlook the harbor, and there was a narrow beach that ran behind the house. But was there a place to dock? She couldn't remember. Snuock had walked her along the top of the bluff once. You could drag a kayak or a canoe onto the sand, but not a fishing boat as big as Quinn's.

Maybe he'd taken the boat and docked it elsewhere, then walked up to the main house, so no one would know that he'd been there.

No.

Whoever had come to Snuock's house had come by car—otherwise, why open the gate?

He'd taken the boat to somewhere else on the island then driven a car over to the manor. Or he hadn't driven, Aunt Margery had.

Then why had he moved the boat at all? Why not leave it where it was, rather than breaking his routine?

Hold on. It couldn't have been Aunt Margery who had driven him. She had been sitting on the beach that night. Angie had seen her sitting next to the small bonfire. Or was she mixing up the two nights?

She tried to relax and let the memories come to her.

No: the first night, on the third, Angie had been wearing a jacket. She had looked out over the beach and zipped it up. The second time she had been wrapped up in the beach blanket. The night of the third, the night that the *Woolgatherer* had been missing from its slip, Aunt Margery had been sitting next to a small bonfire.

Which meant that she couldn't have gone with Quinn.

What if he'd come back, though? He'd taken the boat to another dock, got out, driven a car to Snuock's house, shot him, then come to get Aunt Margery to help him.

Angie tossed back and forth.

But the body had been left on the floor. What would she have helped with? Cleaning up evidence? Wiping off fingerprints and placing the gun in such a way to make it look like a suicide. And she would put herself at risk why? Because she still loved Raymond Quinn.

What time had Angie woken up that night to realize that Aunt Margery wasn't in the house?

One o'clock, she remembered. She rolled over and looked at her clock: it was after that, now.

What time had Snuock been killed? She didn't know.

She couldn't be sure about the beach behind Snuock's house; she couldn't be sure of the time that Snuock had been killed; she couldn't be absolutely sure of the spray of blood that had hit Aunt Margery's dress—one picture wasn't proof enough.

She needed to go back to the house and find out. Probably the study was taped off or locked up. In that case she could ask Valerie, maybe she remembered. Or could be talked into opening the door a crack, so they could peek.

#

In the morning, Aunt Margery's door was closed. Angie could feel her presence in the house. And her purse and shoes were in their normal spots: shoes by the back door, purse hanging from one of the kitchen chairs. Angie started her normal routine then stopped in front of the coffee pot: to make the coffee or not make the coffee? Make the coffee and pretend everything is normal. Or, don't make the coffee and add insult to injury for which she would never be able to forgive herself.

They were two adult women, both single. It was the little things that mattered, that kept the peace and their lives running smoothly.

She would make the coffee.

It wasn't exactly an admission that everything was normal between them, but they were family and that bond trumped anything that threatened to undermine it. She opened the coffee bag and inhaled its rich, nutty roast.

#

She opened the bookstore. Soon, Jo arrived with the day's pastries and the current gossip:

"Everyone wants to know if you're going to close the bookstore."

"What?" Angie put a stack of books on the table in the back and gaped at her friend. "Someone spreading rumors?"

"It's not hard for people to see something is going on between you and your great-aunt. She hasn't been in to the bookstore to help during the afternoons. I opened the shop for you one morning. And you've been closing early and closing for lunch."

"*You* made me do that. And I've done it once!" Angie was incredulous.

"Therefore," Jo said, ignoring Angie's interruption, "the bookstore must be closing."

Angie blew a frustrated raspberry into the air. "I hate gossip."

"You still have to live with it."

"Are there any theories about why any of this is happening?"

Jo tapped one finger on her chin. "I see where you're going with this. No. I haven't heard any theories other than Snuock's raise in rent. I think the consensus is that it was intended to drive Quinn out of business and the rest of us that go under are just collateral damage. So you're the rest of us."

Angie shook her head. "At least there aren't worse rumors going around."

"Yeah, it could absolutely get worse. Any messages you want to pass on? Sometimes it's better to accept that gossip is going to happen and try to put some spin on it."

"You could say…" Angie's mind raced. "You could say that I'm trying to give Aunt Margery a break after the fourth, and that I'm thinking about hiring an assistant so that she can have more time off to enjoy her retirement."

"Ooh," Jo said. "I like that."

"Just don't say that she's sick or anything. She'd hate that."

"Okay. But that won't last forever."

"It will. If I hire an assistant."

"You can't just hire an assistant in order to help with gossip, Angie. It's bad business."

Angie rolled her eyes. For all that Jo thought herself a ruthless business manager, she was the less savvy of the two of them. "I've been thinking about it anyway."

"Why? Aunt Margery does a great job here."

"She does. But we have nobody to help cover us for emergencies, and books are heavy."

"But won't that be...an extra expense?"

Angie's shoulders dropped. "Yes."

"Can you really afford it? *Now*?"

"I can't keep Aunt Margery here forever," she said. "She needs to be able to live her life, not get stuck facilitating mine. She helped me get the bookstore established. Which is more than I could have ever asked of her. But I can't expect that to last. At least I can start planning now to hire summer help, college students to work over the summer during the busiest hours."

"Okay," Jo said. "That almost sounds like you've thought about this."

"Not all the way through. But good enough for gossip, right?"

"Right. So, off the books, how are things going with her?"

"I don't know. We still haven't talked. At least I went home last night, and made her coffee this morning."

Jo shook her head. "And? What else are you going to do about it?"

"I'm...if she doesn't get here by one, I'm going to close up the bookstore again and drive out to Snuock's house."

"Why?"

"There are some things I need to check."

"What?"

Sometimes Jo was just as nosy as Angie. She thought about shaking her head and refusing to tell her—but that would have been hypocritical. She told Jo briefly about the thoughts that circled in her head all night and kept her up.

Jo gave her a strange look. "What if...?"

"What if I'm wrong?"

"Yeah."

"Then I'm wrong," Angie said.

"I don't know if you're right but you're not wrong," Jo said. "*Someone* killed Snuock. And Aunt Margery is acting fishy as hell. If it wasn't her and Quinn, and it wasn't her without Quinn, then why did she have blood all over her clothes? Did she pull over to the side of the road to drag a dying deer out of the way? What?"

Angie's mouth opened. Something had just occurred to her. "Could you swing by my house on your delivery rounds?"

"Sure. Why?"

"I want you to look inside Aunt Margery's car and tell me if there's any blood on the seats, or anything covering them to hide a stain."

#

The hours crept by slowly. Jo called a little while later to report that the inside of Aunt Margery's car was clean, repeat: clean. Not even dust on the front dash. For all that Aunt Margery couldn't be bothered to do, she was a real hound for keeping things tidy. She did most of the cleanup at the house, too. And there were no signs that she had had stains removed—no light spots on the upholstery.

Angie wished that she was more of a Poirot, able to work everything out in her head all at once, instead of with painful, step-by-step slowness. She wanted to be able to have a sudden insight that would unlock all the answers for her. Instead it felt like she was struggling with a stack of corporate analyses, looking at different venture capital possibilities, knowing that they were all risky, but that one of them stuck out as being different than the others, either for better or worse.

And she was going to have to sniff out which that was.

Information. She needed more information.

The problem was too complex for her intuition to figure it out in a snap. All it could do was tell her when something smelled funny. And this smelled funny.

If Aunt Margery had been covered in blood, she would have left traces inside the car, unless she had driven back home naked, used a different car, or picked up a change of clothes.

Angie could think of ways for her to have done all three. She *could* have jumped through a lot of mental hoops and come up with answers for anything. She was creative enough.

But *why*?

A lot of her suppositions served her central premise, which was that Quinn had killed Snuock and her great-aunt had helped him somehow, planned or otherwise, and they were both now trying to cover that up.

If she let that go, what did she have left?

Was she really back to Walter having killed his father?

What about the bloody clothes? Coming up with excuses for her great-aunt to have been burning bloody clothes out on the beach when simply shoving them in the *garbage can* would have done (had the blood been on them for any innocent reason) was a laborious effort.

Her great-aunt was involved. But not the way that Angie thought.

How, though?

How?

Chapter 14

QUESTIONS & ANSWERS

At one p.m., Aunt Margery hadn't shown up. Angie closed the shop, drove to a hamburger-and-ice-cream shop where she had a patty melt and a cherry Coke, then drove out to Snuock Manor.

Her assumptions had been stripped down to nothing but a couple of pieces of burnt clothing and a lot of checkboxes for what could *not* have happened. She had questions to ask, but she didn't even really expect to find answers, at least not ones that would satisfy her.

The gate was closed.

Angie stopped, rolled down her window, and pressed the intercom button. If nobody answered, she would just turn around and go home.

"Yes?"

She was staying. "Valerie? I'd like to ask you a couple of questions."

"You and every reporter from here to Boston."

Angie bit her lip. "I'm sorry. I'll just..."

"Never mind, Angie. I'm on edge. I didn't mean to snap at you. Of course you can come in. I could use someone to talk to about some things, as a matter of fact. I feel like I'm starting to go crazy in here."

"You're not all by yourself, are you?"

"Well, there are the people who come in and take care of the grounds, who don't talk to me, and the housekeeping staff, who I have mostly told that they're not needed for the time being because I...because most of this stuff...because...it would be easier to talk to you if you would just come up the drive, Angie."

The gate opened and Angie drove through. It closed behind her, either to cover up the fact that someone had come through or to make sure that she couldn't escape before Valerie was done with her. She parked in her usual spot behind the main house, then got out and looked around. Valerie was walking toward her from along the bluff, and waved at Angie to come with her.

The two of them walked in silence to the edge of the bluff and looked over.

"Tell me I'm not crazy," Valerie said.

"You're not crazy."

"Thank you. You're seeing what I'm seeing, right?"

The two of them looked down at the harbor, the boats sailing around in it, and the long set of wood stairs leading down from where they were to the beach at the bottom.

"No dock," Angie said.

"Right. *No dock.* I'm not stupid. I've heard the rumors, that Walter didn't kill his father—for a kid who has been spending years trying to make peace between *those* parents, I can't believe that it was him for a second—but that it was Raymond Quinn who did it. Now, I'm not that familiar with Raymond Quinn, but I know that he doesn't have a car—he has a boat and a bicycle. And if he rode a bicycle out here and had to have Alexander open the gate for him, I'll eat my hat, which I will have to go out and purchase because I don't have one."

"And he didn't take his boat out here."

"Where would he dock it? It's not like he *swam* out here, climbed up the hill, and walked dripping into the house. I would have known if that's what had happened."

The two of them watched the waves coming in for a while.

Valerie took a deep breath then turned toward Angie like she was expecting a fight. "I've heard other rumors, too. That Raymond Quinn wasn't the only one out here. That your great-aunt, the one who works with you at the bookstore, helped him."

Angie squeaked, "Where did you hear that from?"

"All I can say is I went into town the other day and people talk. I can understand if that's why you're out here, to put the kibosh on that. I don't know what you think you're going to find that will help you do that, but I can understand."

"I'm glad," Angie said. "Because that's exactly what I'm doing. I have a question...and a favor to ask."

"Ask away. The answer might be no."

"What was the actual time of death? Do you know?"

"Nine-thirty on the night of the third," Valerie said without hesitation.

Angie's mouth dropped open. "What?"

"I didn't stutter. That's what the police told me."

"I know, I just can't...I'd assumed it was later."

"Why?"

Angie shook her head. If Snuock had been killed earlier where would her Aunt have been at the time?

She would have been...

She would have been with Dory, having supper. That's what she'd said.

Except that Dory had said, twice at least, that she and Jo had been having supper together. She'd been covering for Jo's night out with the guy with the mohawk, though. Was Aunt Margery lying because Dory had told her about covering for Jo? If so, all this should take was...

She was forgetting the blood all over the clothes again.

She wanted to forget.

The reservation at Sheldon's had been at nine-thirty, so there was Walter's alibi: Angie and anyone who was at the restaurant that night. She felt like breaking into a dance, except...

Why hadn't he been released?

"What is it?" Valerie asked. "I can see your mind running a mile a minute."

"Walter hasn't been released, has he?"

"Nope. Word is he won't say a word about where he was that night."

"He was with me—at least he was at nine-thirty. We had a reservation at Sheldon's for that time."

Valerie frowned at her. "So you're telling me that he's covering up for someone?"

"But who?"

"The only person I could think of would be his mother."

"Where was she?"

"She won't say," said Angie.

"That's suspicious."

"It is. But then she's pretty eccentric." Angie blinked. "Quinn."

"What's that?"

She waved her hands restlessly. "You can't say anything, but I think she might be sleeping with Raymond Quinn."

Valerie clucked her tongue. "Wouldn't *that* be something. I just assumed that Alexander was off his rocker for threatening to cut off her allowance. But that would do it, all right. As soon as she did anything that threatened his control—and we all know just the mention of Raymond Quinn got under skin—well, forget it, no more cushy life for her. And then, more because she'd been told not to than anything else, she'd have to do it. She'd try not to. But she'd have to do it. That woman is an odd duck, I tell you."

"Yes, I've met her twice and that came through loud and clear. Is there a dock near her house?"

"Her house is right along the water on Smith's Point," Valerie replied. "All she'd have to do is drive out to the docks at the end of Massachusetts Avenue and pick him up."

"And there wouldn't necessarily be any records of him docking there."

"Nope. There's nobody there after dark. As long as he didn't moor there for too long, or he had an agreement with somebody. Or paid cash."

Angie reveled in the back and forth between her and Valerie. It made her think of Holmes and Watson. She felt like they were getting somewhere...until another thought occurred to her:

What if Quinn wasn't involved at all? What if he had an alibi, one he wasn't willing to admit to, in case it got Phyllis cut off from her means of support? And what if Walter was trying to protect his mother, too?

The two of them were back to looking at the water. It was a beautiful July day, the perfect kind of day for standing around and looking down at waves rolling across a beach.

"One more thing," Angie said. "Can I see the study?"

"It's locked."

"I thought so. I want to look at the bloodstain and analyze any kind of spatter. I didn't do such a great job capturing those details with my camera." She hung her head a little ashamedly when she recalled how Valerie had called 911, and she instead had gone straight for her phone's camera.

"There was spatter," Valerie said drily. "I keep having nightmares about trying to clean that room. That wallpaper needs to come out."

"Can I see the room? Like peek through the doorway?"

"No. The door's locked and sealed. I handed over the key. And even if I happened to keep a copy somewhere, they'd know if I opened the door."

"There isn't a video camera in the room or anything?"

"In the study? I wish. Then the police could have just rewound the tapes and found out who'd done it."

"Could you describe it for me, then?"

"I could. But you'd have to tell me why I should, first. Because it sounds like you have a reason that I can't even guess at, and I'd need to know that reason before I'd be willing to help you any further than I already have."

Tell her or don't? Lie? How could she both tell the truth and protect her Aunt Margery?

"Never mind," Angie said. As expected, what she'd found out hadn't given her any of the answers she actually needed. She turned back from the bluff toward her car. Time to go.

"Wait," Valerie said. "You're not the only one with questions, you know."

Angie turned back. "I'm sorry, of course not. Go ahead."

Valerie reached into her pocket and pulled out a scarf. "Have you ever seen this before? It's Phyllis's, isn't it?"

Angie could feel the blood drain from her face. Her mouth went slack with shock.

The scarf matched the dress; the one that Aunt Margery had been burning.

"You recognize it, don't you?" Valerie said. "Admit it. *Whose is this?*"

It was the scarf that they had picked up from a guest room and used to open the door of the study. Angie had completely forgotten about it.

"This is what I used to open the study door," Valerie said. "I shoved it in my pocket. And forgot about it until today when I found it getting dressed. But if it belongs to Phyllis, and she was with Quinn that night...that doesn't make sense. She hasn't been here for years. She and Alexander wouldn't have anything to do with each other face to face. And it wasn't here before Alexander kicked me out of the main house on the third. It had to have shown up after that."

Angie couldn't speak. Her throat had seized up.

"Was this your great-aunt's?" Valerie demanded.

Lie...or tell the truth?

"No," Angie said. "That's not Aunt Margery's."

"You're lying. I can see it on your face. I can hear it in your voice."

"It's not hers," Angie insisted.

"It's one of that crowd. Ruth's then. She's always wearing that hippy clothing."

At just after nine o'clock that night, Angie had been dragging Ruth's heavy bag of trash out to the bin for her. It had been during the frantic rush to close up the bookstore so she could go out with Walter that first night at Sheldon's.

It hadn't been Ruth.

A picture flashed in front of her eyes, and she swayed. Valerie grabbed her by the arm. "Don't faint. Please don't faint. Let's go back in the house and get some water. You haven't been sleeping, have you?"

Angie let Valerie lead her back inside the main house; Valerie opened the fridge and pulled out a bottle of water. Angie sat on one of the kitchen stools around the central island and put her head in her hands. She felt dizzy.

She couldn't say anything until she had decided what to do.

What did she want to have happen?

She didn't want anyone to get hurt. *Someone* was going to get hurt. Conversations flitted through her memory, a line here, a line there. Like a refrain Aunt Margery words marched through her head: "Think about what you would like to have happen before it's too late."

"I have to go," Angie said finally. She hadn't touched the water.

"You have to tell me what's going on," Valerie said. She was using the kind of voice that Dory used on Jo all the time: the "mom" voice.

"No," Angie said. "I'm sorry, Valerie. I don't."

Valerie rolled her eyes. "You're trying to protect your great-aunt. It's obvious. Just say so."

#

As Angie drove back from Snuock Manor, she kept digging her fingernails into the steering wheel and biting the inside of her cheeks.

What she had was circumstantial evidence, at best. But it might be damning: Valerie would probably take the scarf to the police. And the police would run forensics tests on the scarf. All it would take would be one hair, one flake of skin and then everything would be known.

She swung back into town and drove past Aunt Margery's house; the car wasn't in the driveway. And, when she checked, the bookstore wasn't open.

Quinn's boat, the *Woolgatherer*, wasn't there, either.

Angie turned to drive out of town, toward Dory's house. The conspirators were gathering to discuss their strategy as the sharks closed in...

A number of cars were parked in front of Dory Jerritt's house, the one that would eventually just slide into the ocean and disappear. Not the only thing around here on shaky foundations, Angie told herself. She pulled along side the other cars and turned off the engine.

What do you want to have happen?

She didn't know. She wanted...she wanted to be one of the conspirators, one of the trusted few on the inside of a terrible secret. And she wanted to be on the side of truth and justice. She wanted to be able to steer the course of fate away from the shoals of too much justice...just enough justice, and no more. Maybe some mercy.

Her thoughts raced as she walked up the path to the front door, climbed up the three front steps, and knocked.

Raymond Quinn answered. "Go away," he said, and tried to close the door in her face.

But she'd already wedged her foot in the door.

"You have to let me in. Valerie is bound to go to the police."

"She's already been."

"She's going to go again. And this time she's going to take the scarf with her."

"What scarf?"

"The paisley one."

Quinn let out a pair of choice curse words, then opened the door, standing aside for her to pass.

The second of the conspirators, Ruth, met her in the hallway. "Angie, you know that you're only going to make things worse. Go home."

Without a word, Angie turned toward the photographs on the wall and touched the one from the yearbook photo.

Ruth grimaced. "You don't listen, do you?" But she, too, stepped aside.

Angie followed the hall into the living room, with its wood paneling and unexpectedly delicate furniture. Dory and her Aunt Margery were sitting together on the divan, the little coffee tray on the table in front of them. They were both holding coffee cups.

"Agnes," her great-aunt said. "You shouldn't be here. You're not welcome."

"I am," Angie said. "I *am* welcome here. You're my family, and you're just bluffing to protect me. You're raising a lot of bluster to try to scare me off, that's all. But here I am."

Aunt Margery looked at a loss. "Such melodrama."

Angie didn't have entire novels memorized the way her great-aunt did, but that didn't mean she didn't have a line or two up her sleeve. "'It is the custom on the stage in all good, murderous melodramas, to present the tragic and the comic scenes in as regular alteration as the layers of red and white in a side of streaky, well-cured bacon.'"

"Oliver Twist," Aunt Margery said. Her lips, pressed together, as if she were about to burst out with a cry ordering Angie from the room, or in tears, or some other gambit.

Dory put a hand on Aunt Margery's arm. "She won't hurt me," she said, "She's family."

Aunt Margery turned her face to the side, then put her coffee cup on the table and walked away. Tears streaked down her face.

Dory looked perfectly reasonable, perfectly calm.

She patted the cushions beside her. "Sit. Tell me all about it."

Angie sat next to her; the seat was warm from Aunt Margery sitting on it.

"I thought it was Aunt Margery and Raymond Quinn for the longest time," she said. She glanced back over her shoulder. No one else was in the room, but it still felt as though their hushed breaths were hanging over her shoulder.

Dory said, "There aren't many secrets between the four of us. They'll hear what you have to say, but they won't intrude."

That last phrase was tinged with a little bit of *or else*.

"I saw the two of them on the beach, and—"

Dory raised a hand. "That's no place to start, Angie. That's not the beginning—that's the middle. Start at the beginning."

"This goes back so far that I don't know *where* to begin," Angie said.

"A good rule of thumb is to start where you came in. Where it started for you."

"It started for me...with the news that Snuock was going to raise the rent."

She told Dory about it as though Dory had never heard of any of this beforehand, not a single word, as though she hadn't been there—the raise in rent, the way that Snuock had stopped by Pastries & Page-Turners, the tense scene between Dory and Snuock when she had come to the back door while he was still there. Then delivering the books to Snuock and practically begging him to take it easy on the twins.

Then she talked about Aunt Margery telling her that she was going out to supper with Dory on the evening of the third—and the fact that later Dory's story had changed to be an evening spent with her daughter, Jo. But the story hadn't been true: Jo had spent the evening with the guy with the mohawk. Angie's assumption that Dory had been lying for Jo's sake had stuck with her a long time; there hadn't seemed any reason to question it.

Then she described meeting Walter. "He made the reservation for Sheldon's at nine-thirty," she said. "The order of the things I found out is what made it so hard to piece together. Because it was the evening of the fourth, when he was out searching for his mother, that he didn't have an alibi. And by the time that I found out that Snuock had died on the third, I hadn't really been thinking of Walter as a suspect anyway. But now I have that sorted out. He must think that his mother did it; he must think that his silence is a way to protect her, even if it costs him."

"Go on," Dory said.

"Oh—I saw Ruth as we were closing the bookstore. I took out her trash. When I went home, Aunt Margery was there and spoke to me about my date with Walter. But at one in the morning I woke suddenly. She was gone then, and I started to worry. I walked out to the children's beach to check for her. Sometimes she just goes out onto the beach, as you may know, to wait for her pirate, the one who's off with the mermaids. I didn't realize that the pirate was Raymond Quinn until later."

Dory shook her head. When Angie raised an eyebrow, Dory replied, "No, go on. If something needs to be said, I'll say it later."

For the day of the fourth, Angie skipped a lot of the details, mentioning only a few things, like seeing Dory all over the place. The things that had misled her: the emergency Phyllis had called Walter about. Then she told her about delivering the last book and finding Snuock's body.

The scarf.

Dory's eyes narrowed. Angie paused to see if she would say anything...she didn't.

She recounted being questioned first by the police, then later by Detective Bailey, then again by Aunt Margery. Then there was the rumor that Walter wasn't Alexander Snuock's son, and the threat that Phyllis's allowance was going to be cut off. Dory and Aunt Margery feeding her stories about the feud between Quinn and Snuock going all the way back to kindergarten, instead of in high school. Then she'd found the picture on Ruth's wall connecting Dory and Quinn.

A rueful smile crossed Dory's lips, and she glanced toward the hallway.

Angie went over Walter's arrest, how resigned he'd been to his fate. Her throat suddenly tightened and she went hoarse. But she continued...Quinn's anger had misled her, how easy it was for him to say that Snuock deserved to die that night at Sheldon's when everyone had gathered to talk about Snuock's death, and whether that would be the end of the rent increases.

"Later, it almost seemed like he was calling attention to himself on purpose," Angie said. "As if he were trying to misdirect attention from another suspect. It wasn't a big risk for him since he knew that he had Phyllis as an alibi if he needed it; she had been with him. And he could probably find someone who had seen either him or his boat on Smith Point. When it came down to it there was no way he could have landed at Snuock's house. There's no dock nearby, and the gate had been opened, so whoever had killed him had to have come by car."

Dory nodded.

"And then Aunt Margery said something that stuck with me. 'Think about what you would like to have happen, before it's too late.' It's been playing over and over in my head."

"What do you want to have happen?" Dory asked.

"I'll get to that later."

"That's fair."

Angie described how she'd seen Aunt Margery a second time on the beach, this time arguing with Quinn. She had found out then that he had been sleeping with Phyllis. Technically, neither of them had been cheating on anybody, yet it seemed everyone had gotten hurt.

Then there were the burnt clothes.

"That's when I knew that Aunt Margery had to be involved. It almost seemed common knowledge that Raymond Quinn had really murdered Alexander Snuock, and the clothes were proof that Aunt Margery was an accessory to the crime. I flipped."

"And confronted your great-aunt at the bookstore the next day." Dory's eyes were penetrating. She seemed to be waiting, on edge, for a cue.

Angie continued, "Yes, and she made it clear I didn't know what I thought I knew, but she also made it clear that I knew something, and it scared her. She wasn't going to help me put the pieces together, and hasn't talked to me until just now."

Angie glanced anxiously toward the hallway.

"She panicked," Dory said, taking a sip of her coffee. "When she had a moment to think about it, she decided that it was best to keep her distance. The more she discouraged you from sticking your nose into things, the better, that was her reasoning. For your sake and for... everyone else's. But you're tricky, Angie. You were always the quiet one who paid attention—Mickey off in his own little world, Jo charging into things in order to right all the wrongs, and you with your big eyes, watching and giggling. The staying Proutys have always been the observant ones. Some would say, the nosy ones, and now it's gotten you here. Exactly where Margery feared it would."

"I'm not finished," said Angie.

"Oh, well, pardon me. Continue then." Dory took another sip of coffee.

"Phyllis came into the bookstore," Angie said.

"She did?" Dory said.

"Didn't you know that?"

"No! My usual source of inside information had cut herself off from the bookstore, and Ruth didn't happen to notice. And by then Josephine was putting up her defenses, too, because she knew she couldn't tell *me* anything without your Aunt Margery finding out about it, and she's always been far less loyal to me, her mother, than to you."

Angie shook her head. She had known something that the cabal hadn't. That had to be a first.

"Phyllis introduced me to *The Little Grey Lady of the Sea*," Angie said.

"Ah. That's how you found out about all of us and our lovely history." Dory paused. "But how did you find out who wrote it?"

"That's a secret that I'm going to keep." Angie didn't want to reveal Sheldon as her source; she thought it best to stay in his good graces.

"It doesn't matter. I can guess." A slight irritation coated Dory's voice.

"*The Little Grey Lady of the Sea* led me to Miss Mark's literary club, and the literary club led me to the photograph of all of you together. And then there was the photograph at Ruth's of you and Quinn, and you were in a long sundress, a windbreaker, and a scarf."

Dory just stared at her, blankly, with no emotion, no fear.

"I have a question to ask you," Angie couldn't stop now. "What did Alexander Snuock steal from you? What of yours did he take credit for? I've been going over that conversation. We were talking about how it was worse that my ex took credit for the work I did for our company than that he was cheating on me. And you seemed to imply that Alexander had done the same to you."

Dory shook her head.

"May I guess?"

"Later. After you've finished."

"Okay." Angie gathered her forces. " So before I came here tonight, I went to Snuock's to talk to Valerie one more time. She told me that the police confirmed that Snuock had been killed on the third, not the fourth, at nine-thirty at night. So I had to go back over everything and sort it out all over again with Valerie staring at me suspiciously. She said that there were rumors about the murderer being Quinn, and Aunt Margery helping him."

"And you could let Ray take the fall, but not your great-aunt."

“Honestly? Yes.”

“It would break her heart.”

Angie made a face. “Even after this affair with Phyllis?”

“I didn’t say it would be the first time he’s broken her heart.”

“Anyway, that was the point at which Valerie took the scarf out of her pocket and showed it to me. It looked familiar. I realized that it would match the dress if the dress hadn’t been blackened and scrunched up, half-melted. She accused me of trying to protect Aunt Margery. I left without telling her one way or the other. I’m sure she’s gone to the police by now.”

“You never know. What made you come here?”

Angie could practically hear what Dory was thinking: *What made you suspect me?*

“You didn’t have an alibi,” Angie said. “I knew that Jo was with her, uh, gentleman that night. You looked me right in the eyes and told me you were with her.”

“She said she didn’t want you to know.”

“Well, she changed her mind. And the way that you and Snuock confronted each other in my bookstore when he raised the rents, that should have told me something a lot earlier—that the grudge that you had against him wasn’t just about defending your kids, it was something personal. Then the photo with you and Quinn, and knowing that he was cheating on you with my great-aunt. When I found out about the real time of death, it was down to you or Aunt Margery: someone who knew him well enough to get him to let them in. And someone with a grudge.”

“And you weren’t going to let it be your great-aunt.”

“No. I wasn’t. So I had to ask myself again: what did Alexander

Snuock take from you? And I realized that the split between your group of friends was in high school, when you were supposed to be engaged to Raymond Quinn. But you never married him. I thought it was Aunt Margery's fault...but I also knew that Snuock was supposed to never be able to leave anything of Quinn's alone. If Quinn had something, Snuock had to have better."

Angie leaned forward and whispered her revelation, "I think he stole *you.*"

"We all make mistakes," Dory said.

"When I remembered the dress in the photo matching the burnt one, I started putting another scenario together: you invited yourself up to his house 'for old times,' dug that dress out of the closet, and wore it. But I have to know. Why that dress?"

Angie knew that once Dory answered that question there was no turning back, the hypothetical would turn into reality, so she waited patiently for the answer.

Dory took the time such an answer deserved, and then finally said, "Snuock gave it to me. A gift. It was a simple dress, but pretty and whimsical. I kept it all these years as a reminder of how moments of weakness can change the entire trajectory of our lives."

"How so?" asked Angie.

"I was engaged to Quinn and Snuock was able to steal me away. He made me feel beautiful and sought-after. He pried me with gifts like that dress. And eventually I gave in. I betrayed Quinn and turned to Alexander. He turned into an old miser, but there used to be something else to him. And as short-lived as our affair was, it was passionate. Quinn blamed Snuock, of course, not me, and our circle of five was broken. The trajectory of lives was changed that year. Quinn turned to your Aunt Margery for comfort but that didn't last. My passion for Alexander faded and I met Hank, the true love of my life.

I got lucky. I had two beautiful children and shared my life with a wonderful man. Aunt Margery, Quinn and Alexander – their wounds were deeper, their scars harder to hide."

With that admission Angie felt like she had been given a secret key and let into the circle, but it didn't make her happy. There was a cost to this knowledge. Angie had known Dory most of her life, she was her best friend's mom, for a moment she wished she wasn't one of the nosy Proutys. Still, she was going to see this through. "You left the scarf on the floor of the guest room, and then the two of you went into the study for some reason... you argued. Maybe you said some things you didn't mean. One of you picked up the gun. You fought... the gun went off. Blood everywhere, all over your clothes.

"You called my Aunt Margery. She was covering for you that night in case anyone asked where you were. You wanted to make sure Quinn didn't hear about you seeing Snuock, because Quinn still gets angry about anything between you and Snuock—they aren't so different those two. But now you were calling her to help with a situation that had gone horribly wrong.

"Aunt Margery showed up at Snuocks with a change of clothes and a plastic bag. You were shaken up. Maybe one of you wiped the gun and the doorknob for print. You both fled, each in your own car. Neither of you noticed the scarf you'd dropped.

"Aunt Margery waited until she was sure I was asleep, then went out to the beach to light a bonfire as a signal for Quinn to come out and talk to her. He didn't. She was so upset that she'd forgotten about the clothes and didn't burn them that night.

"She had to wait for another night, one where I shouldn't notice she was out. But I noticed, and saw her and Quinn together. She'd started burning the clothes, but Quinn stormed off the beach toward me, and she panicked and left. I went back later, stirred up the ashes, and found them before she could come back out and recover them, or make sure they'd been swept out to sea. Since then everyone's been trying to steer me away from the situation. If I thought that Aunt Margery was involved, then maybe, just maybe, I would leave it alone."

"But you didn't," Dory said.

"I couldn't. I knew just enough to know that if I didn't do something, my great-aunt was going to go to prison."

"And what do you want to do about it now?"

"That's the million-dollar question, isn't it? The police know that Alexander Snuock didn't kill himself, and that he didn't have an accident all alone in his house, cleaning his gun. They're going to find out that Walter wasn't the murderer; he was out in public at the time of his father's death, and eventually that will come out. They'll find out that Quinn and Phyllis were together. They'll find out Aunt Margery's DNA wasn't on that scarf then they'll find out who the scarf belonged to. You can't shift the blame to a new target forever. Someone has to be blamed for the death, and the only logical people are all people you care about. Who do you want it to be? Mickey?"

"He wouldn't fit in the dress. But you haven't answered the question. What do you want to have happen?"

"I want...I want you to go to the police and confess. Tell them that it was an accident."

"Was it an accident?" Dory asked.

The whole house seemed to go still. Angie could hear the wood floors in the hallway creak.

"Yes," Angie said firmly. "You're not the kind of person who kills someone just because they've made a mistake. And what Alexander Snuock did was a mistake. He said to himself, 'That Raymond Quinn and Phyllis Snuock, they've pushed me too far. And now they'll have to pay.' He thought that taking their money away was a fair punishment. It's the only hold he had over them. He was up there, all alone in his house, and he thought, 'You know what will make me feel better? Hurting someone else, and manipulating them so they have to dance to my will.' And that was a mistake. That was how he ended up so alone...and so easy to convince to let you in. He let you in because he thought you might get back together with him, finally, now that Hank was dead for a year."

Dory shivered and rubbed the sides of her arms. "Hank. I miss him so badly."

"I'm sorry. I shouldn't have brought it up."

"No, I agree...that must have been what he was thinking. When Hank first passed, he tried..." She sniffed. "Excuse me, I'll be right back."

She put down her coffee cup and walked down the hallway.

A moment later, Angie heard the front door open, then close. A car engine started then drove away.

She sat shaking on the couch with her hands clenched into fists. All of this because of love...because of mistakes that people made over their stupid money and pride. How disappointed Snuock must have been when he realized that Dory didn't want *him*. She only wanted him not to raise the rent on her children. He'd lost his temper.

It must have been terrifying.

To kill a miser, all you had to do was prove to him once and for all that nobody wanted him, only his money.

Angie closed her eyes and cried. Like a child she tried to hold in the sound and conceal her tears. After a moment someone sat on the couch next to her, the rattan creaked. Angie leaned into her Aunt Margery and they held each other. The heartbreak was almost over.

#

Dory drove back to town slowly, five miles under the speed limit. It was a beautiful day, the kind with a scattering of puffy white clouds across a sky so blue that it seems to take all your cares away.

She was distracted and she didn't want to get in an accident.

The road slowly and regretfully led her car toward the police station. The classical music station played Spanish guitar songs that all sounded like the story of a love that was not meant to be.

It was for the best that it was over; it was for the best that she was going to confess. She had tried to convince herself that Alexander's death hadn't meant anything, or at least that he had deserved it, if anyone did.

But the situation had threatened her best friend—the friend who had taken her fiancé away from her, but Dory could't blame her, they were young, and then she'd gone and fooled herself into thinking she could have an affair with Snuock without any consequences. Then Margery lost Quinn to his own arrogance. And after the affair with Snuock Dory didn't stand a chance of getting Quinn back. Forty years of friendship had eased the quagmire and bitterness of that whole situation.

Quinn. Snuock. They had shaped her youth. But neither man had been Hank Jerritt; neither of them could make up for his loss. She still felt that a hundred times more than she ever would the insult of losing Quinn to her best friend, or the slow drifting apart that she had had with Alexander.

Goodbye, Hank.

Tears welled up in her eyes and she pulled over.

A few minutes later, she was at the police station, sitting across the desk from Detective Bailey.

He stated their names, the date and the time, and said, "You are being recorded. Do you wish to have a lawyer present?"

"No, I'm fine."

She smiled. If Josephine had heard her, she would have railed against her mother and told her never to speak to a police officer without a lawyer present.

"Please tell me what happened, starting on the morning of July third."

She took a deep breath. "I found out that the rents on the properties Alexander Snuock owned were going to be raised significantly, far above the ability of my children, Josephine and Michael Jerritt, to afford as owners of the Nantucket Bakery, about seven hundred dollars a month."

"How did you find out?"

"My daughter, Josephine, told me."

"What did you do when you found out?"

"I drove into town with the intention of discussing the matter with other tenants to find out what the raises in rent would be for them. I wanted to know whether the rents were being raised consistently—or just for my children. Alexander Snuock has had a grudge against me ever since we stopped dating, forty years ago."

Detective Bailey paused for a moment, as if to let that sink in.

"And did you discover whether the raises in rent had been applied fairly?"

"I wouldn't say they were fair..."

The conversation went on for almost two and a half hours. By the end she was hoarse and had described going up to Alexander's mansion in order to confront him.

"And then I parked behind the house," she said, "where my car wouldn't be seen from either the drive or the old carriage house, where I knew Valerie, the housekeeper, would be."

"Could she have heard you arrive?"

"That's possible, although I doubt it. That old carriage house is well built, with solid walls. I'd been there previously and...I'd noted that it was very quiet and isolated."

"All right, you pulled up behind the house, and then what?"

"I went inside."

"Was the door unlocked?"

"Alexander let me in."

Blushing furiously, she told Detective Bailey about her encounter with Alexander, and how he had asked her if her dressing up and seducing him had meant that she was over Hank Jerritt's death.

"And that's when it all fell apart," she said. "I...I hadn't intended for anything to happen. I just got carried away."

"I understand, ma'am," Detective Bailey said, in the same professional voice that he'd used throughout the rest of the interview. "What happened then?"

"We fought. He accused me of trying to use him. I accused him of being nothing more than a heartless miser. He seemed to take it as a personal challenge. He said that the twins would be hearing from him soon. He planned to increase their rent even further. I'm not sure whether he really intended to or not. He might have just said that to make me angry. I followed him from the guest room to the study. By then it was very dark out, and the fireworks were going off outside. I could barely hear them, but I could see the flashes of light from inside the house."

She closed her eyes. The window of the study had faced toward the harbor. The sound of the explosions seemed to echo faintly from every direction—the sky flickered. The lights in the room were dim. Alexander turned on his desk lamp and sat behind the desk, looking up at her with a vicious expression.

"You've never loved me," he had snarled.

She said, because it was *that* kind of fight, "That's right. I only used you to get back at Quinn for cheating on me with Margery."

He sneered. "That arrogant, two-bit pirate. He couldn't even write a decent sonnet."

Dory had almost burst into laughter then. If she had, maybe things would have gone differently. But she had been too angry.

"If you do this to my children, I'll..."

"What? What will you do?"

She was at the other side of the desk then, leaning forward with her fists on the wood. She had worked so hard, for so many years, to keep her family together, to find happiness with Hank. Now she had money, no husband, and her children had been out of the house for years.

She understood how it made the loneliness echo.

She hadn't answered. She *knew* that Alexander was a lonely man. She knew it now in a way she hadn't understood for the previous thirty-odd years. She wanted to make everything better again—not to become a possession of his—not to be tied to him or obligated to him—but he'd spent so long not knowing anything but money and power and how to manipulate people.

"Alexander," she started to say.

His face had turned bright red, the color of a stroke or a heart attack.

He pushed back away from the desk and stumbled, ending up against the countertop under the windows. His hand closed on something.

He raised it toward her. An antique silver-chased pistol, carved silver flowers and vines over the barrel and winding down into the hilt.

She went cold. She was about to be killed by a piece of art.

"Back! You old hag. You are not going to use me." His face was almost purple.

She stepped around the desk toward him. She needed to convince him to put it down—

He charged toward her. His face looked completely insane. "How *dare* you make this about you and your cheap, piece of trash children from that cheap, piece of trash husband—"

She shoved him. He swung the pistol toward her head.

No, no, no...!

She swung her arms, caught the pistol. Alexander had been a miser, deteriorating in his house for the last forty years. She had worked on the docks. She grabbed the pistol. He tried to keep it. The trigger guard jammed onto his finger. He shouted in pain.

"Let go!" they both shouted.

She twisted him around in a hold and pried the gun off his finger. She threw it on the floor and he shoved her out of the way to try to get at it.

She kicked his hand but he kept his grip. Then he was up again, and she reached toward the gun, both holding onto it, pushing it this way then that, until there was that shock of sound. A sound she'd only heard in movies. It was more deafening than she'd ever imagined. At first she thought it was thunder, or fireworks.

The lights outside flashed.

Her ears rang.

His face was red with rage. He rose to his feet and charged toward her. She thought, Oh thank God, it missed. She pushed him back and he fell down.

But when he hit the floor she noticed her dress was covered in blood. Maybe wearing that particular dress had been the thing that had taken them all too far. She'd had it for thirty years or more. She couldn't remember the last time she had worn it, except that it must have been with him.

Alexander rolled on his side and groaned. "Leave me alone, you bitch. Just leave me alone."

Her knees were sticky and wet with blood. She'd been kneeling in it. She watched its crimson color spread..

"I'm sorry," she said. "It was an accident."

"I don't forgive you. I don't." His voice went faint. "At least..."

And then he stopped, like the last tick of a clock. She sat next to him unable to move or think for who knows how long. When she finally got up off the floor she thought, At least the bottoms of my shoes don't have blood on them. At least I don't have to track blood all the way out of the house.

"And then?" Detective Bailey said.

"And then I went down to the beach and burned my clothes. I had a change in the trunk," she lied.

Chapter 15

FORGIVENESS

Later, when she found out, Jo was furious that Angie hadn't called her to help confront her mother. Mickey...was more understanding.

"You would have been all confrontational," he said, "and it would have made everything worse."

"She was using me as her alibi!"

"Why not? You were using her as yours."

"That's not the same thing. In my case a man didn't die!"

Mickey was the voice of the calm, "It's over now, Jo. You know she didn't mean it. It was an accident." That was all he had to say before shifting his attention to Angie and other topics. "So, custom cupcakes? Are you trying to tell me that it's a mistake to specialize in pastries? I should do cupcakes?"

Jo paced back and forth across the kitchen, kicking her apron up in a petulant fluff with every step.

"No," said Angie, "I'm just saying that you should play around with the idea and see whether you can make any extra profit. The custom cupcakes in Manhattan were always *really* expensive."

"Ehhh...Manhattan," Mickey said, waving one hand, a quick disregard for Manhattan's pomp and circumstance.

"Don't even think about blowing the cupcake idea off," Jo said. "I happen to have a boyfriend in Manhattan now."

Mickey rolled his eyes. "I have dishes to do. And it looks like I am going to have some cupcakes to design and make."

Jo grinned eat-to-ear and gave Mickey a pat on the back. "That's my bro."

He headed to the sink.

Jo sat on one of the baker's tables; Angie sat next to her. The two of them stared out the front windows. Jo had closed the bakery as soon as Angie had walked through the front door. She let out a deep breath and leaned against Angie's shoulder.

"What are we going to do?"

"About what?"

"About Mom. About the rent. About you getting an assistant. About Walter. About everything. About my boyfriend."

"Boyfriend?"

"I finally swallowed my pride and texted him. He couldn't figure out which number was mine. He'd randomly drunk dialed a couple of people that night, apparently, hoping he'd find me."

"But called all the wrong numbers and got yelled at."

"He's an idiot."

"But is he worth dating? That's the question."

Jo bobbed her head from side to side as if considering it. "I want...I want everything to work the way I want it to, with no hiccups or interruptions or logic or fairness or reason. I have a selfish heart that way."

"Does that mean you forgive me?"

"As long as I get to keep giving you crap about it whenever I'm annoyed at you."

"That's fair."

#

The only part of the story that had to be changed was that Dory hadn't called Aunt Margery in. She had taken a couple of garbage bags from the kitchen, put them over her seat, and driven home, where she had destroyed the clothing all on her own.

That was the price everyone in the circle had to pay for Dory coming clean: they all had to lie to keep her best friend out of it.

Detective Bailey seemed to accept the story. It was the smart thing to do, the easier, less complicated way.

Walter was released the same day Dory confessed, and he offered to pay her legal fees.

Dory tried to refuse, but when Jo stepped into a room with her, half an hour later they came out, their faces streaked with tears, and she had changed her tune.

Mistakes were made. Under the advice of Walter's lawyers Dory pleaded involuntary manslaughter. Whatever had happened, happened in the heat of passion, and the death was unintended. The consensus among Walter's friends in the legal business was that it would be judged an accident, and the charges dismissed. Dory's actions could be considered self-defense; it would be hard to prove that they weren't.

Angie spent the day after the confession on tenterhooks at the bookstore. Every move Aunt Margery made, Angie jumped about a mile in the air. She bent over backward making sure Aunt Margery had everything she needed. She blabbed about getting an assistant about half a dozen times. It was going to take some time to get their relationship back on track.

Aunt Margery made a phone call. Angie chatted to customers.

Half an hour later, Walter arrived with a picnic basket and orders from Aunt Margery to keep Angie out of the bookstore until after closing time. He drove her to, of all places, his father's house, where they spread the blanket out on the bluff overlooking the harbor.

"Why here?" she asked.

"Because one, we won't be interrupted, and two, we won't have to use one of the beach outhouses. Which can get gross. "

She laughed. "I have no idea what you're talking about."

He poured her a glass of wine, and they toasted each other. "To sharing afternoons in the sand and sun," he said.

"I'll drink to that." His words were a warm blanket of security.

After a few moments watching the sunlight glimmer and dance across the water, and sailboats tack back and forth in the distance, Walter said, "I really came here to start mourning my father."

"I know," she said. "It's strange, I feel like I have to get to know my great-aunt all over again. I know her, but I don't know her. Everything is a little different now. Honestly, it's kind of difficult thinking of her as a tragic, romantic figure, who loved not wisely but too well."

"I can see that."

"And you're trying to come to grips with the fact that your father..."

She drifted off. "Sorry," she said. She had her own theories, but she didn't want to put words in his mouth, either.

"That my father was a miser? Sure, but really he was just a deeply flawed human being. Mom's always been more three-dimensional to me. You know, kind of weird, but sharp, too. Like you say, a romantic figure in some ways."

Angie's impression of Phyllis was not flattering; she hadn't learned enough about Phyllis to see her as more than just plain odd, so she skipped saying that, too.

"So, the million-dollar question," she said.

"Am I going to raise the rents?" Walter said.

"*Nooo*," Angie said. "Are you going to *stay*?"

"Don't you care about the rents?" The surprise on his face bordered on shock.

"Of course I do," she said. "But the rents are one thing and you're another. I care about you." Well, there, she'd put herself out on a limb, now what?

He kept a steady gaze on her; his lips gave just a twitch of a smile. She couldn't handle the suspense

"You're killing me," she said.

His smile broke into a laugh. And just to torture her, it seemed, he lifted the wine and poured them each a little more. Then he built her cute little cracker sandwich stacks with cheese and fig jam, and little sprigs of thyme on top, and then laid them on a small plate.

She pulled at tufts of grass, trying to keep her cool. He moved closer to her.

"I didn't think I was going to stay when I got here this summer. I do have things back in Manhattan that I can't just pull up stakes and leave behind. Some people I care about would get hurt. So I think I'm going to be running back and forth for a while." He took his fingers and pushed her hair behind her ears. "But you Ms. Prouty have given me serious reason to reconsider staying."

"I don't know. That puts a lot of pressure on a girl."

"What do you mean you don't know?" His eyes danced all over her face, searching. She kind of enjoyed seeing him off balance.

"This girl needs a little more than that."

"How about this." He leaned in and kissed her. His lips were warm and soft, and they felt just right against hers.

"That helps." She cut him a sly grin. "So, we're dating?"

He laughed out loud. "We most certainly are."

Angie laughed with him. She took in the wide-open blue sky above them and the leafy trees at the edge of the bluff. In front of them Nantucket Harbor was picture-perfect, shaker homes all neatly tucked away just beyond the marina, and seagulls swooping down, a sanctuary in all that blue ocean. After all that had happened, she couldn't help but feel fortunate in this moment, and that it was going to be a good day.

~

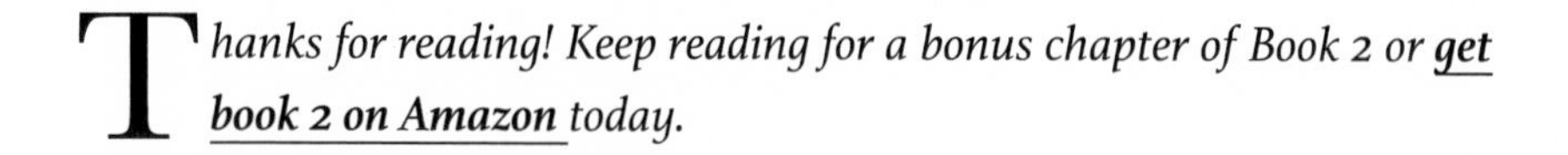

T*hanks for reading! Keep reading for a bonus chapter of Book 2 or* ***get book 2 on Amazon*** *today.*

THANK YOU!

Thank you so much for reading Crime & Nourishment! Just like baking the perfect cake, the process of publishing this book required inspired prose chefs, delightful literary ingredients and lots of patience. It was not quite easy as pie but we feel that the final product really takes the cake. We hope you agree.

Books with reviews sell like hotcakes so we'd love it if you would be kind enough to take two minutes right now to leave a review of the book. To leave a review simply visit the **book page on Amazon** and click the button that says *Write a Customer Review.*

Crime & Nourishment is book 1 of the Angie Prouty Nantucket Mysteries, book 2 is available now! Get **Prize and Prejudice** from Amazon today, or turn the page to read Chapter 1 from Prize and Prejudice.

Thank you for joining us on this adventure!

- The Team Behind Miranda Sweet

BOOK 2: PRIZE AND PREJUDICE

Chapter 1: The Treasure Hunt

Weekends after Thanksgiving on Nantucket had always been a little bit nuts, honestly. Not as nutty as they were on the mainland, but not without a handful of slivered almonds now and then. Shoppers came over on the ferries and wandered the well-decorated island in a holiday mood. Light poles were wrapped with tinsel. Parking meters received big red bows. Lit Christmas trees floated in rowboats in the water. A giant wreath was attached to the Brant Point Lighthouse. Carols echoed from every shop as the tourists flowed through the town, buying caramels and ornaments and antiques, waking up to the smell of maple syrup and pomegranate waffles at the B&Bs, and listening to Santa's belly-laugh as he and Mrs. Claus took an honorary stroll at the Nantucket Hotel.

But weekdays?

Weekdays were supposed to be dead so that Angie would have time to deal with all the mail-order and Internet books that she needed to have shipped ASAP from her bookstore, Pastries & Page-Turners, in time for Christmas.

Instead, on a Tuesday, the bookstore was positively packed with shoppers.

"Oh, Aunt Margery," she said. "I almost resent the fact that Walter came up with such a brilliant idea for whipping up business on the island during the holiday season. Couldn't he have waited until after Christmas?"

"You don't mean that," Aunt Margery said.

Angie sighed. She didn't, really she didn't. She was so far into the black at this point that there was no question that she and Aunt Margery would be able to afford a vacation to the Mediterranean in January.

"You're right." She would suck it up and, in fact, feel grateful for the business. It wasn't just Pastries & Page-Turners that Walter's treasure hunt idea was benefitting, but the whole island.

Angie had moved the register off the tall side counter and onto an antique desk so that Aunt Margery, who was really her great-aunt, could check out customers without having to stand on her feet all day long. Angie was handling customer requests and other emergency issues. The café counter was being managed by Angie's first non-relative employee, a young woman named Janet Hennery who made decent espresso drinks without getting flustered, even if the line almost stretched out the door.

The front door jingled, and Angie crossed her fingers that it was from a customer leaving—not a new one coming in.

"Hello?"

But the voice was coming from the back of the shop, not the front.

Angie sidled through the customers, excusing herself as she went, and came face to face with Mickey Jerritt, who was holding a large flat white paperboard box.

"Hello!" He exclaimed when he saw her. "Backup pastry delivery, courtesy of my sister, who sends her regrets as she cannot get away from the shop at the moment."

"You still have extra pastries?" Angie asked incredulously. Mikey and his twin sister, Josephine, were the owners of the nearby Nantucket Bakery, a popular local destination.

"I think the general idea was that after I delivered a bunch of them to you, we wouldn't," Mickey said. "And then we could close up."

"I'll take 'em," Angie announced without hesitation.

"Nothing fancy, just cupcakes with frosting and sprinkles."

"I could sell sugar cookies dusted with green sugar at this point. Everyone seems to be starving tonight!"

She looked for a path through the crowd toward the café counter that would be wide enough to accommodate the enormous box, but there wasn't one. Mickey grasped the situation and hoisted the box overhead, then said loudly, "Excuse me! Sweets coming through!"

People laughed, but they scooted out of his way. Angie followed in his wake and held the box while he unloaded the cupcakes into the display case.

"White with red jimmies is for red velvet. Red with white jimmies is for white peppermint with pomegranate jam. Green with black jimmies is for chocolate peppermint with mint crème. White with green jimmies is for rosemary mint."

"Rosemary mint?"

"Everyone went nuts for them at the bakery this morning, so I thought I'd try them out on you. White with the little blue snowflakes is blueberry crunch. The ones with the tan frosting with tiny marshmallows are burnt marshmallow and bourbon. Chocolate frosting with tiny marshmallows is hot chocolate, and the ones with the red and green candied fruit on the gold-dusted frosting is fruitcake."

Angie laughed. "Fruitcake! I don't think anyone will buy those."

"They're not real fruitcake. Just the best rum-soaked cupcakes with candied fruit that you'll ever eat. Just because you can use some fruitcakes to beat up burglars doesn't mean that they're all bad. *Mine* are great."

"I'm sure. I'll save one to split with Aunt Margery and let you know how it tastes."

He grinned at her, then hefted the empty box back over head.

"Thanks, Mickey," she said. "Janet? Did you catch all that?"

The espresso machine screeched as Janet pulled a double shot. "I think so!" she shouted over the noise.

Angie sighed in relief, then worked her way through the crowd toward a waving customer who wanted to know if she had any books on the lost Monet of Nantucket. About a dozen other customers hushed as they heard the question.

If she'd *had* such a book, then there would have been a stampede for it.

She said, "I'm sorry, nobody has written one. Maybe after the painting is found!"

Several people laughed.

"And I'm afraid we're completely out of books on Monet at the moment, although we have an entire section on the history of the island…"

She led them toward the correct shelves, which were already surrounded by treasure hunters.

Walter Snuock had inherited half the island of Nantucket after his father's death in July. His father had been about to raise the rents on all his properties in order to bring them in line with market value. Walter was trying a different method of achieving prosperity by raising the rent only slightly…and by hosting a treasure hunt to find a lost painting, a genuine Monet that had disappeared almost a hundred years ago.

There was a hundred-thousand-dollar reward for the painting, which was estimated to be worth over one and a half million dollars. None of the residents of Nantucket or their families or employees could win the reward—it had to be a tourist. If the painting was found, it would be put on public display at the Chamber of Commerce.

The result was that the whole *island* had gone completely nuts every day of the week so far.

She simultaneously wanted to hug Walter and shake him.

But he had been making himself scarce on the mainland lately. He had stirred the pot, then left everyone else behind to deal with the rolling boil. He was a lawyer in Manhattan, and he had several cases to wrap up before he could spend more time on the island.

And with her.

~

At eleven o'clock, Angie closed the doors and locked up. Her eyes were burning and her legs ached. She should have gone straight to the boxes she was packing and worked on them, but instead she found a comfortable overstuffed chair in the café area and sat down.

A cappuccino appeared in front of her. Or at least, something resembling a cappuccino. She could tell just by looking at it that there wasn't enough foam mixed in with the milk and espresso, but it was an improvement over Janet's early attempts.

Angie smiled up at Janet. "Thank you. Why don't you finish closing the coffee bar and take off for home?"

"I think I will. What a day. I hope they find that picture soon, don't you? Or at least that people get bored with coming over here to hunt for it. If it were something you could find in a single afternoon, someone would have found it already. I actually had someone ask me if he could start pulling up floorboards to look!"

Aunt Margery claimed the chair next to Angie's. "I had someone try to pull the drawers out of the desk...while I was sitting at it!"

The three of them shook their heads. The treasure hunt seemed to be giving the normally-polite tourists justification for acting like children.

A soft "*meow?*" echoed from the back of the shop. Angie turned around and spotted Captain Parfait, the store kitty. He was a large tortoiseshell cat with a scar over one eye, a ragged ear, and a limp. Angie had adopted him within a week of opening the bookstore, and fortunately, he seemed content with his limited territory. Although he did have a tendency to shred anything that looked even vaguely mouselike that he could get his paws on.

Angie clucked her tongue and scratched her knee, which was her way of inviting Captain Parfait to climb up on her lap. He did so, headbutting her chin before settling down to be petted.

Janet reached over, gave Captain Parfait a scratch behind the ears, then headed back to the café area.

"What do you have left to do?" Aunt Margery asked.

"Everything. I wasn't able to get to a single thing."

"Why don't you go home and get some sleep, then come in early?"

Aunt Margery was infamous for staying up late and sleeping in. Some days, she wouldn't appear until after noon. Not that Angie could complain. She was lucky to have Aunt Margery's cool head as well as her expertise at reading people. And, after the events of last July, she was lucky to have Aunt Margery's affection and friendship.

Angie a.k.a. "Agatha Mary Clarissa Christie" Prouty's first murder case had nearly caused a family tragedy, as Aunt Margery had set herself on one side and Angie on the other.

But that was over now.

No more murders. She just didn't have time for them.

"I can't," she told her great-aunt. "I have too much to do, and I don't want you carrying all those heavy boxes of books around."

"I can carry 'em," Janet announced.

"You're going *home*," Angie said. "Remember?"

Janet laughed. "Actually, I'm going out with some friends."

"Then that's even more important." Angie dug her fingers into Captain Parfait's fur and gave him deep, massage-like scratches. He stretched out all four paws until his toes were splayed. He purred loudly.

Then, after a few seconds, he hopped down and began to prowl around the shop. He could only take so much spoiling before he had to get away and pretend that he was the fierce and untamed hunter of his youth.

Angie rose from her chair and tried to shake off the feeling that she was at least a hundred years old. Maybe the cappuccino would help. She took an experimental sip and gave Janet a thumbs-up. Not bad. Then she carried her cup into the back office, which also served as the stock room, and booted up the computer.

The priority tonight, she decided, would be to get the boxes of books packed and ready for the delivery driver to pick them up in the morning. The rest of her tasks would just have to wait. She would keep her fingers crossed that someone would find the painting soon. Of course, right after the painting was found, the island would be even *more* crowded as people came to see it, but at least there would be an end in sight.

She checked over her orders, printed out the receipts, and started pulling books out of boxes. She stacked some books on her order table and the rest on a sheet on the floor, placing receipts on top of the completed piles. She'd be surprised if she was out of the store before midnight.

Putting it all in order was deeply satisfying, and she found herself whistling happily as she worked.

Suddenly she came upon the slip for Reed Edgerton, who was ordering, not bestsellers or thrillers or cozy mysteries, but books on the subject of Nantucket. She chuckled. He was an art professor at Harvard who taught Eighteenth and Nineteenth century art history. His favorite painter was J.M.W. Turner, a unique Cockney artist who had worked in the Nineteenth century. Turner's work wasn't entirely to Angie's tastes, but she couldn't seem to stop staring at it, either. She had stopped to look at one of his paintings at the Boston Museum of Fine Arts and couldn't seem to look away.

From behind her, someone had said, "Eerie, isn't it?"

She had almost jumped a mile. "Yes, actually, although I'm not quite sure why."

She found herself facing a shorter man with broad shoulders, light-brown skin, and a beard speckled with white. His hair had receded like the tides and left a gray-pebbled bald spot behind. He smiled.

"You haven't read the title yet, have you?"

She hadn't. She leaned forward and read the brass plate at the bottom of the large oil painting. It read, *Slave Ship (Slavers Throwing overboard the Dead and Dying—Typhoon coming on), 1840.*

She looked at the painting again and gasped. Amidst the beautiful colors and atmosphere of the painting were what she had assumed were fish or birds at first glance—hands reaching out of the water, and links from several enormous iron chains.

"The painting has been carefully composed so that it strikes almost every viewer in the same manner," the man said. "The sunlight in the middle of the frame draws the eye. Then, one might glance at what is in the foreground, but the mind processes it as merely fish or birds, and so one moves to the ship in the background. 'Ah,' one says to oneself, 'a storm is coming.' It is only upon further reflection—or upon seeing the title—that other details pop out, and the true meaning of the picture appears."

She shook her head. "It's distressing. And moving."

He smiled. "I'm glad to hear it. Let me take you to the café for a cup of coffee or tea, and give you a moment to sit and recover."

"Thank you."

Only after she was comfortably seated and had a cup of coffee in front of her had he introduced himself as Professor Reed Edgerton of Harvard. They had enjoyed a pleasant chat and had exchanged emails.

Angie wouldn't have exactly called him a close friend, but she always looked forward to exchanging emails and messages with him over books and paintings. She usually stocked her art section based on his recommendations, and they had met at the museum for several art shows ranging from Matisse and Botticelli to photographs from the Lodz Ghetto by Henryk Ross. She always felt that talking to him improved her ability to see the world, in one way or another.

She pulled the books he was looking for and sat down to write him an email.

Reed, I saw your order on Nantucket books come in! Does this mean that you're coming to the island to look for the lost Monet??? Please do! I'd love to see you. Should I hold the books here or send them to you in Boston?

She stepped out of the stock room to find Aunt Margery squinting at the computer in front of her, reconciling the drawer and the receipts with what she'd rung up. Janet had left long ago. She'd probably said a cheerful "goodnight," too which Angie had completely missed.

"Aunt Margery?"

"Yes?"

"Thank you."

She smiled. "I wasn't going to sleep anyway. Did you need something?"

"It looks like Professor Edgerton, that art professor from Harvard, is coming out for the treasure hunt. And I want to know if you're fine with putting him up in our guest room."

"Certainly," her great-aunt said. "But remember, he's a very private man. I suspect that he's found another place to stay. Don't be too disappointed if he says he'd rather not."

Angie laughed. "You make it sound like I'm eight years old and having my first sleepover with my friends."

"'Some day you will be old enough to start reading fairy tales again,'" quoted Aunt Margery. "C.S. Lewis."

"I'll ask, anyway."

She added the invitation as a P.S. to her email and hit send, then cheerfully worked on packing up the rest of the books.

Get the book on Amazon to keep Reading

ABOUT THE AUTHOR

Miranda Sweet is a collaboration of authors, writers, editors, creatives, and cozy-mystery lovers. Miranda Sweet novels can be relied upon for classic cozy themes, settings and characters. Her books are best enjoyed with a hot beverage and a pastry.

To learn more about Miranda Sweet and get free books and recipes visit **MirandaSweet.com**

Made in United States
North Haven, CT
18 February 2022

16234029R00157